THERE WILL BE BEARS

THERE WILL BE BEARS

RYAN GEBHART

CANDLEWICK PRESS

First edition 2014

Library of Congress Catalog Card Number 2013946620
ISBN 978-0-7636-6521-0

14 15 16 17 18 19 BVG 10 9 8 7 6 5 4 3 2 1

Printed in Berryville, VA, U.S.A.

This book was typeset in Warnock.

Candlewick Press
99 Dover Street
Somerville, Massachusetts 02144

visit us at www.candlewick.com

For Grandma and Papa

I Drink Half a Liter of Prune Juice and Use the Neighbor's Toilet for Two Hours

Country Orchard Prune Juice, reads the label on the plastic jug in front of me. They say this thick, nasty-looking sludge is a potent laxative. Well, I'm about to drink the whole thing.

I heard somewhere that courage means being afraid of something and doing it anyway. I never thought I would be so frightened by a fruit juice, but my heart is pounding and my palms are sweaty. As far as I know, no one has ever OD'd on prunes.

Google, please don't let me down on this one.

Gramps sits across from me at the kitchen table, his fingers tapping against his own jug, checking the birdsong clock above the sink.

In fifty-four seconds, it will be six o'clock.

Tick.

In fifty-three seconds, the Canada goose will honk.

Tick.

In fifty-two seconds, Gramps and I will each be chugging a liter of prune juice to completion.

Pruning, Gramps calls it. Before he goes on his yearly elk hunt, he prunes so he'll be ready to face the wilderness. He says it's good for the digestive tract, puts hair on your chest, and makes you feel like a new man. And for my thirteenth birthday, Mom and Dad promised I'd get to join him this weekend. We're going to the Bridger-Teton National Forest in Wyoming, and I've been waiting for this trip all year. Not only do I get to hunt with the coolest old guy in Colorado, but this will also finally be my chance to see a grizzly bear in the flesh. I've been obsessed with them since I saw the Timothy Treadwell documentary. He lived with the bears for thirteen summers, until one finally ate him. It was so cool. But Gramps says that if I want to go, I have to prune with him.

Mom would never let me prune with Gramps — she thinks it's immature and disgusting — but Mom's not here. And what Mom doesn't know won't hurt her. It might back up the toilet, but I'll just blame that on Ashley.

"You ready, Tyson?"

This is it. And to my own surprise, I'm not that scared. The Canada goose honks, my eyes close, and I'm choking the stuff down. My eyes are watering and my throat gets tight and I'm just about to refund all over the table when Gramps gives a satisfied sigh.

"That's the stuff." He wipes his mouth with his forearm.

I can only finish half of my jug.

Now, your typical old person just drinks a small glass of prune juice with his toast and soft-boiled egg in the morning to stay regular, but Grandpa Gene is insane in the good kind of way. He wears his beat-up cowboy hat to church and sits in the front row. And he'll dance with any woman at the Rodeo Tavern. It doesn't matter if she's some hot woman in her twenties or some fatty in her fifties. He just loves to dance.

Gramps is pretty much my best friend. Well, Brighton is *technically* my best friend, but lately he's been busy with football practice and hanging out with his new girlfriend from American Civ. The last time we actually did something was in July, when we sang karaoke for his birthday. He has a game tonight, so at least I'll be able to see him then.

"Now what?" I ask, a sour aftertaste in my mouth and a purplish-brown mystery sitting low in my stomach.

With one hand against the table, Gramps hoists himself up. "We watch *Wheel of Fortune*."

I follow him into the living room. There are still a couple of unpacked boxes from when me, Mom, Dad, and Ashley moved into his house last month. It already feels like home, all old and broken in. Heck, we've spent every holiday here since Ashley was born. I know everything about this house, from the crawl space in the basement to the picture of Michael Jordan slam-dunking in the bathroom.

In *the* bathroom. As in *one*.

There's only one bathroom in Gramps's house.

Why didn't it occur to me before? What are we going to do?

"What time is your friend's game tonight?" he asks. He makes a relaxed groan, deflating into his reclining chair.

"Um, what are we going to do about the bathroom situation?"

"What do you mean?"

"Who gets the bathroom?"

With a devilish grin, he says, "Whoever is faster."

My stomach gurgles like someone just flushed a toilet. "Huh?"

"Your grandmother and I pruned twice a year. Once in

the spring, once in the fall. We watched *Wheel of Fortune* and *Jeopardy!*, and then we raced to the bathroom."

"What does the other person do?"

"They make do. Now, hush."

This is the most horrifying episode of *Wheel of Fortune* ever. How can people be solving puzzles at a time like this? Who cares about a new car or a ten-thousand-dollar prize?

After sixty agonizing minutes, I've become an overfilled water balloon hovering above a needle, ready to explode with prune juice and bad news.

I can't make any sudden movements.

Gramps lowers the leg rest and gets into position.

We both eye the closed door at the end of the hallway.

As soon as *Jeopardy!* ends, we make a break for it, rushing for the bathroom like football players trying to recover a fumble. He stiff-arms me with his left hand, and I fall to the ground, using every muscle to hold back this cat-4 hurricane inside of me. Gramps may be bigger, but I squeeze my way underneath him and I'm just about to make it to the bathroom when —

"What the heck?" Dad stops both of us when he opens the door going to the garage.

"We were just —"

Gramps closes the bathroom door behind him. I hear the horrifying click of the lock and the bathroom fan turning on.

"Dude, you cheated!"

Dad says, "Tyson, what's going on?"

I bolt out the front door, my butt cheeks clenched tight. Where do I do the deed? The Privetts' house or the Castillos' house? Who would be more offended by me barging in and tearing up their bathroom?

The Privetts.

So I run toward the Privetts' house.

Mr. Privett looks at me all weird as he opens his front door. He can't really help it when his turtleneck is swallowing his face like a snake with its jaw unhinged.

He says, "Ty. What can I do for you?"

Oh, man. Cat-5! I break past him and hurry for the bathroom, locking the door behind me. I drop trou and . . . dang, Mr. Privett has a pretty solid setup in here. There's a whole stack of mags, really fruity potpourri, and this toilet paper is way better than what we have at Gramps's place.

Now I can just sit back and relax.

He knocks. "Tyson—"

Guh. "I'll be out in a sec."

In here, I don't have a care in the world. In here, I can read *Better Homes and Gardens* to my heart's content.

He knocks again.

"I already told you, I'll be out in a second."

"Tyson Eugene Driggs, it's your father. You can't go barging into Mr. Privett's house."

"Sorry, Dad. I had to use the bathroom, and Gramps was using ours."

"Then you shouldn't have drunk an entire bottle of prune juice."

"I didn't."

"Don't lie to me."

"I only drank half."

There is a long pause, and I fill the silence by misting some Mountain Spring air freshener.

He says, "You and I are going to have a little discussion."

"What? Why?"

"Meet me in the kitchen at seven thirty. We'll talk then."

"I'm a little busy right now. You better reschedule for eight thirty."

"Tyson," he says, then draws out a pause. "You're not going hunting this weekend."

CHAPTER 2

Me and Gramps Make Our Hands into Bear Claws and Growl

Dad takes a seat next to Mom at the kitchen table, looking all parental and stern. But he can't bring me down. My body hasn't felt this clean in a long time. I guess a diet consisting mostly of Fruit Roll-Ups, cereal, and pizza will back a guy up.

He says, "We need to talk about your grandfather."

I raise an eyebrow. I thought this conversation was going to be about me. "Why?"

"I don't want you pruning with him again."

"But it's good for you. Prunes are high in antioxidants and potassium."

"Your grandfather has some health issues, you know. High blood pressure, bad kidneys—"

"Yeah, but now he has a perfectly clean digestive tract."

Mom snickers, but Dad maintains his death glare.

"And I don't want you two hunting, either."

"Why not?"

Mom says, "Honey, with what happened to that guy from Portland, it's just not safe."

"What guy from Portland?"

"This tourist was hiking near the Tetons just three days ago, and for no reason a grizzly ripped his arm off. He's lucky he's even alive."

"That's fierce."

"It's true! The story is all over the news."

"Whatever. Gramps has encountered bears before and it wasn't a big deal."

"That was a long time ago," Dad says. "He's seventy-seven now. You think he can outrun a bear at his age?"

"He beat me to the bathroom."

Dad rubs his temples, then his eyes. "Maybe next year."

That's his way of saying we're never going.

"Dad, you know how much this means to me."

"Since when have you been interested in hunting?"

"I like hunting. I have all the Great American Hunter games, and Gramps has taken me to the shooting range a bunch of times. He says I'm a really good shot. And I love nature. I got all the *Planet Earth* DVDs."

"Do you really want to kill an animal?" Mom says.

"Yeah. I do."

"Why?"

"It's those video games," Dad says in his know-it-all way. "Always shooting something."

"No! No, it's not that. It's not about killing. It's about . . . I don't know. Something else." I slouch back and mutter, "We didn't go on a trip this summer."

"What's that got to do with anything?"

Every summer all six of us would pile into Grandma's minivan and head for the west coast. My favorite trip was the one when we drove to Los Angeles, then traveled the entire Pacific Coast Highway up to San Francisco. With everyone crammed together and all tired and stinky, I felt like a bear cub in a den. When we got a flat tire, Gramps fixed it. When I wanted a slice of gas station pizza, Dad paid for it. When I got angry at Ashley for farting and blaming it on me, Mom yelled at us and Grandma laughed. I loved our vacations.

But I don't say any of that. It's not going to change their minds.

Dad goes, "It's getting late. Don't you have an American Civilization test tomorrow?"

"Yes."

"Well, move along, then."

If Gramps wants to take me hunting, then what gives Dad the right to stop him? I mean, this is Gramps's house. He let us move in here when Dad lost his job and couldn't keep up with the house payments and had to declare bankruptcy.

I open my American Civ book to the chapter "US–Great Britain Relations, Pre–Revolutionary War." After I read through it, I answer the questions at the end of the chapter and get over half of them wrong.

God, I can never get the details down. What sucks is that the details are what Ms. Hoole tests us on. The doctor says it's because of ADD or ADHD or something. He says I can't focus and I get overexcited, and Brighton says that explains my obsession with grizzly bears and Taylor Swift.

There's a knock on my door, which means Gramps. Mom and Dad never knock.

"Come in."

He sits beside me on my bed, a book in his hand. "Hey, bud. Sorry I got you into trouble."

"It's not your fault Dad's so lame."

"Don't be so hard on him."

Now I feel kinda bad, but only for a second. "So we're not going on our hunting trip?"

"We're going. Yes, sir, you and I are going to get a six-point. A real trophy bull. Maybe we'll go next weekend when your father is in a better mood."

"Pinkie swear?" I hold out my little finger.

"I *bear swear.*"

"Huh?"

"Do this with your hands."

He makes his hands into bear claws, and I do the same thing. He interlocks his fingers with mine and then he growls, violently shaking my hands.

"Never break a bear swear," he says. I have no idea what it means, but I can't stop laughing.

He hands me a worn hardcover book with a picture of a bear titled *Grizzly Bears of Northwest Wyoming.* "I found this in the attic; thought you might like to take a look. I know how much you love bears."

A grizz shows me his teeth from the cover as he roars. They're stained brown with the blood of the less fortunate. His eyes are soulless little black dots. He eats, and he doesn't care what.

God, I'd give anything to see a grizz up close.

I say, "What's your best bear story?"

"I've never told it before?"

"You always said I was too young."

"Ah, well, you're thirteen now. In a lot of cultures, that's the year boys become men."

There's no way I'm a man. I mean, I've never even kissed a girl.

"So my best bear story? Well, that's gotta be when my hunting guide Brendan Rien and I were out tracking an elk herd back in, uh . . . 2003. The timber got too thick for the horses, so we tied them to a tree and moved on foot. We didn't get no elk that morning, but when we returned, you wouldn't believe it — all that was left of our horses were two heads dangling from the ropes, still tied to the trees."

"Whoa. What happened?"

"A grizz happened."

"He ate *two* horses? What?"

He shakes his head. "It was a she. About ten yards away, we saw two piles of dirt. There was blood everywhere and it stank like you wouldn't believe. She buried their bodies. I mean, can you imagine the strength it would take? Digging holes for two horses?"

"But why would she bury them?"

"She was waiting for them to spoil. Grizzly bears like their meat rotten."

A chill falls down my body and freezes up my stomach. I just got an all-too-real picture in my head of rotting horses and I can't get it out.

"That's bold," I say, like I have no problem with rotting bodies or dirt puddled with horse blood. But I have to think of something else. I try to force a picture of that new girl in choir class, but the image of a horse's head is stuck in my brain.

I fake a laugh and say, "You know, she wouldn't have had to kill the horses if there'd been a pizza place around."

Gramps shakes his head. "You really like pizza, don't you?"

"You really like The Weather Channel. No judge."

"You're going to learn quite a bit. This is why I hunt out of the Tetons every year."

"Dad says you have to watch your blood pressure."

"I've been hunting elk, deer, and black bear ever since I was thirteen. I don't have to watch nothing."

"You've been hunting since you were my age?"

"Yup. Your great-grandfather first took me to the Tetons when I was thirteen. And he was thirteen when his father took him. It's a family tradition — all men hunt and field-dress an elk when they turn thirteen."

"Did Dad?"

"Well, he killed an elk, a sad-looking four-point no bigger than a mule deer. But he left the field dressing to me."

"No way! Dad went *hunting*? How come he never told me?"

Gramps laughs. "There's a lot of responsibility that comes with killing an animal. More than your father could handle."

"I can handle it."

"He couldn't stand the sight of blood."

"That's 'cause Dad's weak."

He smiles. "Looks like you missed your friend's game. Did you ask him how it went?"

"Brighton isn't answering his phone, and the Internet's down. I'll just talk to him at school tomorrow."

"Nah, let's go see him now."

"Really?"

"Yeah, I'll drive you. I should have told you not to make other plans when pruning."

"But what about Dad?"

"He already went to bed."

I slide on my shoes. Whatever health problem Gramps has, it can't be that bad. He's the same guy he's always been. Still hunting elk, still pruning, and he doesn't treat me like a child the way Mom and Dad do.

I say, "And then maybe we could order a pizza."

Gramps shakes his head. "We'll make a man out of you yet."

· CHAPTER 3 ·

It Turns Out My Best Friend
Is Actually a Yamhole

I follow Gramps down the staircase. He bought this house with Grandma the year Ashley was born and the rest of us were living on the other end of town. Sure, all the other homes in the neighborhood are nicer and newer, but it's like someone took a cookie cutter and baked the exact same two-story cube a hundred times over.

Gramps's house has a soul. The pine trees in his front yard are huge, while all the neighbors just have saplings being held up by twine and metal rods. Some yards have sod that didn't take, and now there are all these patches of yellow grass everywhere.

I close the door and head to Gramps's pickup.

Gramps dials the radio knob to 96.9—KBCR Big Country Radio—and they're playing Willie Nelson and Merle Haggard singing one of Grandma's favorite songs.

I slouch back and imagine wearing Gramps's cowboy hat, driving in my pickup through the canyon to work another day at Henry Feed and Tractor Supply in Hayden. One arm rests on the windowsill, and I eat a Fruit Roll-Up my old lady packed, because she knows how I think Fruit Roll-Ups are the cat's pajamas, as Grandma would say.

We pull into Bright's driveway, and the light is on in his bedroom, just above the garage. With Gramps waiting in the truck, I ring the doorbell. Chloe starts barking.

Bright's mom answers the door, and Chloe rushes out to snort at my ankles, wagging her tail. Her eyeballs bug out of her smashed pug face, making her look like a mouse caught in a trap.

"Tyson, hello. What are you doing over here so late?" His mom sounds so formal, with her thick British accent. Bright was born in England and moved to Colorado in the first grade, but the only time he sounds remotely British anymore is when he laughs.

"Is Brighton home?"

"Let me fetch him."

It sounds like he trips and comes tumbling down the staircase. But he appears in one piece, wearing a green polo and expensive jeans. Or as I like to call them, his fancy pants.

"Hey, Ty." He coaxes Chloe into the house and closes the door behind him. "What's up?"

"I just wanted to see how your game went. Did you win?"

He scratches at his buzzed head. Bright and his teammates shaved their heads at the beginning of the season as some good-luck thing. He looks so much older without his shaggy hair.

"Nah, we lost."

"What was the score?"

"Thirty-one to thirty-three."

"Hey, at least it was close. Did you kick any field goals?"

"A twenty-five yarder and a nineteen yarder."

"Twenty-five yards? Good job, football bear."

He makes a little grin. "I missed the third kick from fifteen yards and lost us the game."

"It happens. So, hey, me and my gramps aren't going hunting until next weekend. You want to hang out tomorrow afternoon? It's supposed to snow. Maybe we could go sledding at Snowshoe."

He shakes his head, eyes to the ground. "I might be going skiing with some of the guys on the team."

"Oh," I say. I get this feeling in my chest. It's like a pain, but not really. I mean, I've seen this coming since summer. Bright's becoming one of the popular guys.

I can already imagine him going to parties and "forgetting" to invite me, and then the next day in the halls, kids will come up to him saying stuff I won't understand. I'll ask Bright what they're talking about, and he'll say, *"Oh, it's nothing. You had to be there."*

Pretty soon I'm going to be just some other kid he nods at in American Civ. Pretty soon I'm going to go from having one friend to having zero friends.

It feels like something is pushing up against my rib cage.

"That's cool," I say. "And sorry I couldn't make it to your game tonight. Something came up."

"What's that?"

"I was taking a dump at the neighbor's house." I'm trying so hard not to cry, because Bright making new friends is a stupid reason to cry. It's not like anyone died. I'm just being all emotional. So I laugh instead. "I drank a bunch of prune juice with my gramps, and dude, have you ever tried that stuff? It works."

He's not even paying attention. He's just checking his phone.

"Who are you talking to?" I say.

"Mika."

"Mikachu!" I say in my Pikachu voice, and Bright barely smiles. "What's she saying?"

"She's just talking about how Amanda Morgan brought this ridiculous sign to the game for Nico."

"Oh."

He laughs. "You had to be there."

A bolt of panic strikes me.

"I'll see your next game," I say. "I promise."

"I should probably get back to studying for Hoole's test. See ya later, Ty." And then he goes inside and locks the door.

I get back in the truck.

"Is everything okay?" Gramps asks.

"Whatever." I turn to him and say, "Let's go over to the water tower."

"Maybe it's best if we went back home. It's getting late."

I slouch in my seat, my teeth clenched. I'm funner than the football kids, but after all these years, why doesn't Bright know that?

Driving down the street, Gramps says, "Okay, just this one time."

He flicks his turn signal and takes a right onto Shady Lane, toward the hills, the warehouses, the highway, and the old water tower.

· CHAPTER 4 ·

Gramps Gets Pulled Over
and I Eat Some Skittles

Gramps pulls in front of the only gas station on Shady Lane. It has bars on the windows and cameras perched on the roof. We walk in, a bell chimes, and I casually check myself out in the security monitor.

I head for the fridges lining the back wall. I scan through the selections until I find the red can with the insane cartoon bird. RoadRunner Energy Drink. It's got ginseng, taurine, caffeine, and my mouth is watering just thinking about that sour tingle on the insides of my cheeks.

I don't want to think about Brighton. I mean, I knew him long before Mika and his football friends. I met him in first grade when Ms. Virost sat him next to me, and oh, my God, he had the most ridiculous booger in his nose.

Heh. I remember him picking his nose, then he showed me the booger on his fingertip.

"You want to eat it?" he said. "It's got vitamin B."

"Gross." I got out of my seat.

"The B stands for *booger!*"

He started chasing me around the desks like we were in an intense game of duck, duck, goose. I wailed like a girl as he wrestled me to the ground.

"Eat my booger!" he said, and back then he had a full-on British accent.

"Never!" I cried like a determined soldier in an already lost battle. I was using all my strength to fight off this disgusting kid beneath the chalkboard, but he was one of the stronger first-graders that played T-ball.

Soon we were inseparable. We'd ride our bikes to the water tower every day after school. We'd climb to the top and eat snow, or talk about stupid stuff, or see how far we could throw rocks. I pretended I was a grizzly named Pizza Bear defending America from the invading Gorlaks. Bright was my trusty sidekick, Booger Bear 5000.

No one else would talk to him because he was the new kid with a funny accent. He worked so hard to sound American so everyone would stop calling him a wiener. But I didn't care. He seemed cool enough.

I hand the cashier my drink and a bag of Skittles. Gramps puts a bag of peanuts and a huge beer on the counter, which is odd because I haven't seen him drink in years. The cashier puts his stuff in one bag and mine in another. His eyebrows are narrowed, as if Gramps is a creeper giving candy to some random kid.

"Have a good night," the cashier says.

When we're out the door, I say, "What was that guy's deal?"

"Don't mind him."

As we're driving away, the guy gets on his cell phone. Oh, my God, is he for real? He's actually calling the police.

I pop the top to my drink. It's tart and eye-opening and strawberry flavored. I say, "Some of the kids at school think it's weird that we hang out."

"Do *you*?"

"Nah, I love it when you take me to the Tavern. You got skills when it comes to the ladies."

We drive beneath the highway overpass, and on the other side, the water tower appears at the top of a hill. It's different coming here without Bright. It's abandoned and dark, and the metal looks cold.

I say, "Maybe you could teach me some of your pickup lines."

"You got a girlfriend?"

"No. But there's this girl named Karen in my choir class. She just moved here from Texas."

"A Texas girl, eh?" Gramps parks his truck past the broken gate and the barely readable No Trespassing sign, in a bunch of weeds growing from the abandoned parking lot. There's a little bit of wind, and the air is heavy, as if it wants to snow. "I met myself a girl from Abilene once, before your grandmother. Dorothy McCoy. Must have been fifty-nine years ago."

"What should I say to her?"

"You just need to be yourself."

That's horrible advice. Be myself? If any girl saw the things I do when I'm alone — when I'm *really* myself — she would never date me. I get excited when I scrape my elbow, because that means in a week I'll have a scab to pick. And if I had the money, I'd get a one-hundred-gallon aquarium and just go to town. Newts, live plants, discus and angelfish, and maybe a small school of neon tetras and a sucker fish to keep everything clean.

I walk to the ladder and grab the bottom rung, but then I let go. For a second I imagine climbing to the top the way me and Bright used to. But that part of my life when we protected the world from the Gorlaks is over. Bright's voice is deeper now, he's got peach fuzz above his lip, and he makes out with Mika outside of Ms. Hoole's class all the time. He'll never throw rocks with me again.

Gramps sits with his back to the rusted metal, his beer in a brown paper bag by his side. His skin and clothes are yellow from the lights. And he looks sad, the way he shells his peanuts and stares at the ground.

"Everything okay?" I say.

"Oh, I'm fine. Just don't tell your father I was drinking and eating peanuts tonight."

I sit by his side in a patch of dead grass. "Why can't I tell him that?"

"I'm supposed to be watching my sodium." He twists open his beer and gulps it down as if he's dying of thirst. He wipes the foam dribbling down his chin. It's just . . . this isn't right, the fact that he's drinking in front of me.

"Is something on your mind?"

He belches. "Nothing you ought to worry yourself about." But with his grim, rumbling tone, I can't help but worry. He takes another swig and says, "Your grandmother was very proud of you, you know."

He's trying to change the subject.

"Proud of me? I was nine when she died. Why? Was it because I made some fierce macaroni art?"

I laugh. Gramps does not.

He says, "She was so proud of you because you didn't care."

"Huh?"

"You were friends with all the other kids in your pre-school. You didn't care who they were; you just wanted to play KerPlunk."

"So what was it like when you were a kid? Was everything in black and white and did kids wear suits and ties to school? Were you not allowed to play KerPlunk?"

I finally get a laugh out of him, but it isn't very rewarding when it's followed by an outburst of tears. There isn't anything more horrifying than an old man crying. It's just something Gramps doesn't do. He didn't even cry at Grandma's funeral. He simply put a rose on her coffin before they lowered it, then walked away with a poker face.

Something must be really wrong.

He looks at me with his eyes all red and says, "I'm glad we're going to have one more trip together, just you and I."

The wind dies. A few flakes of snow drift down like ash. What does he mean? Is he dying?

Even though I'm right by his side, he's never looked more alone.

Headlights appear at the end of the road beneath the highway overpass. I picture the Grim Reaper in the driver's seat, his sickle sticking out the window, coming to take Gramps away.

He jumps to his feet and hides his bottle and paper bag in the dead weeds.

We get in the truck and he pulls past the gate in reverse. That's when I see the car blocking our way. It's a Ford Crown Victoria. It's white. It has a spotlight next to the rearview mirror and lights on the roof.

Gramps lowers his window. A cop shines her flashlight into the truck.

"Evening, officer," Gramps says.

She says, "A little late to be out in this part of town, don't you think?"

"I was taking him to his friend's house, but we got lost." Gramps points his thumb at me, and I offer a wave. His voice is a pitch higher than usual and it sounds fake, like he's trying to pretend he's not nervous.

"We got a phone call this evening; guy at the gas station said he wanted me to check you out. He said you were hanging out with a young boy and purchasing alcohol."

"Yes, officer. This is Tyson. My grandson. The beer — obviously — was for me."

"Have you been drinking tonight?"

"No." He pauses like he's choking. "Well, only the one."

"Have you been drinking *and* driving?"

"No!" he squeals. I've never heard Gramps sound so . . . pathetic.

"Would you mind stepping out of the truck?"

"Absolutely, officer."

I remain still, drinking my RoadRunner and trying my hardest to act like everything is perfectly cool and normal as he goes through a sobriety test. But this is so messed up.

Another cop car appears behind the first. A minute passes and Gramps has his finger touching the tip of his nose when someone taps on my window. I lower it.

"How's it going, son?" This cop rests his arms on the windowsill and looks around inside.

With a mouthful of Skittles, I say, "Good."

"Mind if I see your beverage?"

I hand it over and he smells it. "You're going to be up all night drinking this stuff."

"I got a test tomorrow."

Gramps returns. He struggles to put on his seat belt, his breathing uncomfortably heavy.

"Did you get a ticket?" I ask.

He makes a wheezing cough from deep in his lungs.

"I blew under the limit. You doing okay over there, Mr. Pizza Bear?"

I want to ask him what's going on, but there's no need. He's sick or dying and he doesn't want to tell me. He restarts the truck, then gives me this disgusting happy look, like I can't figure out the obvious.

I breathe in the dry heat from the vents.

"Yeah," I say. "It's all good."

CHAPTER 5

I Murder a Newt

Gramps pulls into the driveway and the cop parks next to us. She walks with us to the front door.

The porch light turns on, and Dad appears, half awake.

"What in the heck is going on?"

With a hand on my shoulder, the cop goes, "Are you the father of this young gentleman?"

"Yes."

"It seemed a little late for these two to be driving to Shady Lane."

Dad's eyes get wide. He clears his throat and says, "Officer, thank you very much for escorting them home."

To my surprise, Dad doesn't ground me. He just says he needs to have a talk with Gramps, so I go to my room. I take my slimy little newt from his aquarium, plop down on my bed, and put him on my chest to roam around. But he just sits there, his little green head perked up, staring at the wall.

I sigh.

"Hey, there, Jar Jar Newtingston. Did you have a good day?"

Jar Jar wanders up to my neck, his cold body tickling my skin. I place him on my comforter and pet his head with my index finger.

"Did you eat all your newt food? You're looking a little skinny, you know."

Jar Jar is getting dry. I put him back in his tank, and he hurries to take a soak.

"Sorry about that, bud."

I stumble onto my bed and grab the book Gramps gave me — *Grizzly Bears of Northwest Wyoming.* I open it to the introduction:

During the postglacial period, the grizzly bears' natural range covered all of the western United States and Canada, extending as far east as Pennsylvania and as far south as central Mexico. Today, their numbers are limited to Alaska, western Canada, and small pockets in Montana and northwest Wyoming.

I yawn, my eyelids heavy. It's three a.m. and the Road-Runner is beginning to run its course. I'm exhausted after all that pruning today. I flip through the pages.

Contrary to grizzlies' gruesome reputation, 80 to 90 percent of their diet consists of vegetation. In the parks of Yellowstone and the Grand Tetons, the average bear spends most of its day grazing on berries or whitebark pine nuts. When plant resources are low, grizzlies are known to hunt and kill large game, such as elk, deer, and even black bears. However, grizzlies prefer eating carrion left from a hunter or another animal rather than expend energy killing on their own.

My alarm goes off before I realize I'd even fallen asleep. It's six thirty.

Oh, no, Jar Jar's light is still on! I must have left it on all night.

I check the thermometer.

Eighty-five degrees! Oh, crap. Everyone knows that the

sustainable water temperature for a newt ranges from seventy-two to seventy-six degrees. Above or below that and they could . . .

I tap on the glass. His motionless body sways in the water. I take him out, and he doesn't move. He's dead.

No. I cannot deal with this now.

Mom opens my door. "Time to get up."

"Don't you guys ever knock?" I put Jar Jar's body back in the tank, sling my backpack across my shoulder, and storm past her.

"Aren't you going to change and take a shower? That's the same outfit you wore yesterday."

"I don't care."

"What about breakfast?"

I hate eating breakfast in the morning. Cereal is for after school, dinner, after dinner, and before bed only.

"Tyson, your coat!"

I slam the door, and jeez, I really should have grabbed my coat. Snow is falling in wet, heavy clumps and soaking into my shirt, but I can't go back now. I'm making a point. And that point is — just everyone shut up and leave me alone.

I arrive at the front doors an hour early, and the janitor Mr. Colby is mopping the floor. He smiles and lets me in.

"Thanks."

I feel bad because my footsteps leave muddy slush on his clean floor. I go to the cafeteria and toss my backpack on a table. Except for the occasional echo, this place couldn't get more quiet. This is the perfect opportunity to cram for my test.

I grab my phone and check Bright's status.

Last night he posted: *I kicked two field goals! Still lost tho :(*

And then a bunch of girls in our grade left a comment about how he's such a good kicker or how cute he looks with his buzzed hair — it's all so lame. They think kicking field goals is impressive? Whatever. I'm going to Wyoming to be a hunter. That'll prove I'm a more dominant male than Bright. While I'll be providing meat and fur for Karen, what will Bright have to offer Mika? An extra three points?

So after third-period art — we're working with charcoal, and I did a drawing of a bear kicking a football — my clothes have finally dried off and I'm starting to feel normal again. Then I enter Ms. Hoole's class and right away something feels different.

Even though Brighton's been dating Mika since the first week of school, he still always sits next to me. We don't have assigned seats, but after a while we assigned our own. Today he's sitting by Mika. Her smile is so big that her braces glisten from four rows away.

I don't want to care. I drew the football-kicking bear for him.

In the middle of the regular pre-class commotion, Timmy, one of Bright's lamer football buddies, snatches the drawing from me, unfolds it, and looks at it with a scrunched face.

"Gay," he says.

"Give that back."

"You have a crush on Bright."

My insides burn with rage that he would even think that. I have to make the best comeback ever.

"That's totally stupid," I say.

"This bear . . . Look, it even has Bright's number on the jersey."

"So? Give it back."

I swipe and get a fistful of ripped drawing when Ms. Hoole enters.

"Tyson," she says, singling me out even though practically everyone is acting up. My face gets warm. "Take a seat."

She stands in front of her desk, a stack of tests in hand.

I see Bright glancing over, rolling his eyes. Ashamed of me.

Whatever. Just focus on this test, and get out of here as soon as possible.

The entire test is multiple choice and fill-in-the-blanks. Questions about names and places I won't remember a year from now.

Why can't Ms. Hoole test me on which years Gramps served in the military?

1951 to 1952. He was part of the U.S. Second Infantry Division.

In which battle was he shot in the thigh?

The Battle of Chipyong-ni, located in the South Korean province of Gyeonggi-do.

I hand in my test. I already know I failed.

Snow is still falling on my walk home, and my hands are stuffed in my pockets. It's not that cold, but since I'm not wearing a jacket, the wind bites through my wet long-sleeved shirt. Mika's mom offers me a ride, but Bright's in the car and I know he thinks I'll embarrass him. So I say no. Besides, I like being the first to make tracks in the snow.

It's also Friday. Yay.

When I get home, Gramps's truck is gone. There's just a pair of tire tracks in the snow.

I stomp my shoes clean on the welcome mat. "Mom? I'm home."

Mom is sitting on the sofa, staring at the television, but the television isn't on.

"Where'd Gramps go?"

"Tyson, I need to talk to you."

"I'm sorry about last night. I know I shouldn't have gone —"

"It's about your grandfather."

I pause. My mind starts going crazy, and my breath gets real short. "Did he die?"

Her eyes get big and she does these quick little head shakes. "Oh, no. He just — no, he's getting older, and you know, people his age sometimes need a little help."

I get ahold of my breath, but my heart still races. "Is he sick? He looks different."

She clears her throat. "It's just with your father finally getting more shifts at the Hampton Inn and me getting my nursing degree, we need someone to take care of him. This is a very normal thing."

"You're getting your degree online. You're home all the time. And what does 'this' mean?"

"Your father and your gramps went to this really nice place up in Rock Springs. The Sunrise Village Nursing Home."

"A *nursing* home? What? Why—why did they go up there?"

Tears fill her eyes, and then she says, "He's moving there."

CHAPTER 6

I Order the Nothing
with a Side of Nothing

I don't want to cry or yell at Mom. I don't want to punch a hole in a wall or have a hug. I just want to know why Gramps didn't tell me something was wrong with him. Does he think I can't handle bad news?

The truth is, I do want to cry my face off, yell all the bad words at Mom, punch *five* holes in the wall . . . and I desperately need a hug. Gramps moved three hours away, and he didn't even tell me.

Frustration and sadness build up behind my eyes, but I can't cry. That's what little kids do, and little kids are told Santa Claus flies in a magical sleigh and his elves build us Nintendo Wiis in their workshop. They're told babies come from a stork. They're told Gramps isn't dying; he's just feeling a little under the weather.

It's one thing for Mom and Dad to treat me like a kid — they're stupid. But Gramps couldn't tell me?

Mom pulls me in for a hug. With my teeth clenched, I shove her away. "Get off."

The front door closes. Ashley's in the hallway, hanging up her jacket and kicking off her boots.

"Hi, Mom. Hi, Tyson," she says.

I go, "Mom and Dad put Gramps in a nursing home."

She comes in, wearing old jeans and a University of Colorado sweatshirt that aren't cooperating with her growth spurt. She makes a sad face, and it's so fake. "That's awful. Mom, what are we having for dinner?"

"Chicken stir-fry."

I can't stand the way Ashley pretends like she's some angsty teenager even though she's only eleven. She really doesn't care that Gramps is sick?

My hand squeezes into a fist, and I punch the wall. I imagine the drywall crumbling down with my unstoppable force, but I don't even make a dent.

Pain explodes inside my knuckles, and I let out a sound that's half roar, half screech.

"Tyson!" Mom yells. "What has gotten into you?"

I'm so angry! It's like someone is feeding me electricity through a wire connected to my chest.

I breathe through my nose. "When are we going to see Gramps?"

"Next weekend. Your father is working tomorrow and Sunday, and I have a test to study for. Will you please settle down?"

Completely unfazed, Ashley says, "Can we have something else? We had chicken last Friday. I'm so sick of chicken."

"I could pick up McDonald's."

"Get me a ten-piece Chicken McNugget with barbeque sauce and a Coke." Ashley vanishes upstairs. She doesn't care that we just lost a member of the family. She doesn't care about *anything*. Ever since we moved here, she's just been hiding in her room.

"Whatever," I say. "I'm going sledding."

"What about dinner?"

"Get me the nothing with a side of nothing." As Mom is hurling more questions at me, I just say my "uh-huhs" and my "yeahs" and play the role of the kid who doesn't care.

"Tyson, come back here. Don't you want to talk about this?"

"No."

I go upstairs, get my phone, and message Bright.

Want to go sledding? I say.

Within seconds he messages back: *Going to steamboat.*
Right.

Karen's online, but I'm not friends with her yet, and my heart speeds up just thinking about sending her a message.

Everyone thinks I'm a kid? Yeah, well, does a kid message a girl?

With the blinking cursor, I write into the box by her profile picture. She's with her two older brothers at a Houston Astros game. She's holding a red snow cone.

I type: *Hey its tyson . . . im in choir class with you first period. I like snow cones too.*

That's stupid. What's she going to say back? *Yeah, snow cones rock!!! You're cute ;)*

I delete my message and turn off my phone. No one ever gives me winky smiley faces. Girls like boys who are cool. They like funny boys or boys who play football.

I'm invisible to girls.

Whatever. Who needs winky smiley faces? Who needs friends or girlfriends? Everyone else gets in the way of what I want to do — Bright would rather play football and do the whole "normal" thing. He thinks we're too old to be sledding. It's just parents and little kids at Snowshoe Hill.

I fish Jar Jar's body out with my little green net, put him

in a Baggie, and carefully stuff him in my jacket pocket. He deserves a proper burial.

I've had Jar Jar Newtingston for five years. Brighton got him for me as a birthday present in third grade, and he named him Jar Jar because he was all into Episode 1 of the Star Wars movies and Jar Jar Binks was his favorite character. But if anyone asks him now about Episode 1, he'll say it's stupid, just because that's what everyone says.

All dressed up in my gear, I get my sled from the garage.

"Mom? Can you drive me to Snowshoe?"

She dabs the corner of her eye with a tissue. "Okay."

She backs the minivan out of the garage. The snow is already starting to melt. By tomorrow, it'll all be gone. By Monday, it'll probably be warm again.

The drive is deathly silent — we don't speak, and Mom has a habit of keeping the radio off.

The snow over at Snowshoe isn't that good. The sun has turned it into a slushy, muddy mess, but at least there isn't a soul out here. All I want is to be outside and alone.

"I'll be back at six to pick you up."

"Thanks."

As soon as she disappears, I reach into my coat pocket

and pull out the plastic Baggie with Jar Jar in it. This isn't just the death of a pet; it's the end of an era.

I scoop out a clump of mud with my hand, place him in the hole, and pat the mud on top of him.

Maybe I should move on like Brighton did. Join the drama or the outdoor club. Find new friends. It can't be that hard. People gain and lose friends all the time.

With my sled tucked beneath my arm, I huff up to the top of the hill, struggling to keep my balance, because the ground is really slippery and the soles of my boots are caked in mud that looks like chocolate frosting. I have on three layers of clothes right now, and it's complete over-kill. But Mom always says that since the weather changes every five minutes, I need to dress prepared.

I bust out of my winter clothing and end up in just my long-sleeved shirt and snow pants. I leave my stuff on top of the hill, sit Indian-style in my plastic sled, and with my hands in the snow, I give my best push. Halfway down the hill, my sled stops.

If I were a year younger and hanging out with Brighton, we'd be laughing about how we're stuck in the mud. But now he's in Steamboat Springs with his cool new friends, and they're probably laughing and talking about boobs or backflips as they soak in a hot tub.

Is he really happy he's not hanging out with me anymore? Will he ever invite me into his new group? Would I even want to be in it?

I lug my sled back to the top.

"You think we'll get our six-point this season?" I say out loud, but I already know the answer. Gramps is seventy-seven and in a nursing home.

Wow, I can't believe he's already that old. Are everyone's lives on fast-forward?

What does he have? Alzheimer's disease? Nah, can't be. He's totally with it. Maybe he's got some kind of cancer. If he told me he had cancer, I wouldn't cry. Would I?

God, I need to stop thinking about this.

I shove off. For a second, my hands are up. I'm getting some serious speed, and when I hit an unexpected bump, I clutch onto the sides of my sled, but I go tumbling out. Dizzy and laughing, I get to my feet. Four high-school kids in the distance point at me and laugh.

I gather my sled and my hat and do one last run. It sucks not having any friends.

I should get Gramps something so he knows I haven't forgotten about our bear swear. I'll get him a card and a stuffed elk. And maybe I can put some red food coloring on its temple, as if it got shot in the head.

When Mom picks me up, I throw out the idea, except for the fake-blood part.

"I think that would be a lovely gesture," she says.

At the mall gift shop, I find a smiling stuffed elk, and after browsing over a million sappy cards with poems and cursive writing—the kind you'd get someone on their deathbed—I grab the perfect one.

On the front it says: *I was looking for the perfect kind of cake to cheer you up . . .*

I open it and there's a picture of a buff dude with his shirt off. The caption says: *. . . so I got you a beefcake.*

Gramps is going to hate this.

It's perfect.

I pay for the card and the stuffed animal and I'm ready to get out of the mall, but then we pass the Halloween store.

A lady dressed as a witch has two full-size bear costumes in her hands, debating where they should go on display.

Oh, my God, they're so nasty. It's like she's holding up two actual skinned bears. They're like some old-school outfit pagans would wear. The upper jaw would hang over my head like a hat, and the rest I'd wear like a fur coat. And those claws must be three inches long!

I have to get it. Every Halloween me and Bright go all out on our costumes. We're a legend around school. Even if he doesn't dress up with me this year, this would definitely solidify my reputation.

"You're not getting those hideous things," Mom says, escorting me out. "Don't spend your money on something you'll only wear once."

"How much did you spend on your wedding dress?"
She laughs.

When we get home, I go up to my room to write in the card. I've been thinking about what I want to say to Gramps. Do I ask him what's wrong, or why he doesn't trust me?

Nah, I'll save the serious stuff for when I see him.

Dear Gramps,
I hope you like the stuffed elk. We'll kill a real
one before the season ends. I bear swear!
  I love you, Gramps!
    — Tyson

P.S. Did you know they named an olive oil after
you? It's called Extra Virgin :]

CHAPTER 7

There Will Be Bears

I really doubt that Gramps and I are still going to the Grand Tetons. I know Gramps said you never break a bear swear, but we only have two more weekends before elk season ends, and he lives in a nursing home now. And even if we somehow found a way to get him out of there, should we? He might be too sick to handle the wilderness. I mean, this could actually kill him.

On Saturday morning, when I get back from dropping off my package with the card and the stuffed elk at the post office, there's an envelope on the kitchen table. My name's on the front next to a really crude drawing of a bear paw print.

Inside is a letter and a newspaper clipping.

Second Bear Attack in Bridger-Teton This Month

A sixteen-year-old girl from Oklahoma was airlifted out of the park Wednesday afternoon after a grizzly bear reportedly attacked, breaking both her legs. The incident occurred at Hackamore Creek, two miles from another attack last week in which a Portland man lost his arm. Local authorities believe the same bear was involved in both incidents. The Forest Service is cautioning visitors to the park not to cook food with lingering smells, to make constant sounds when traveling through the woods, and to always carry a can of bear mace.

And then I read the letter:

> *Tyson,*
> *Pack all my hunting stuff when you come here next weekend. The key to the gun safe is in my bottom dresser drawer. Don't tell your parents we're going. Looks like you might get to see your bear after all. Cool, huh?*

Mom and Dad would freak if they found out Gramps told me where he keeps the key. When we moved here last month, him and Dad got in a fight about how he kept his rifles displayed above the TV, so they went fifty-fifty on a gun safe. It's not like I don't know how to handle a rifle, and I would never treat it like a toy. At the shooting range, Gramps always stressed the importance of gun safety. But Dad thinks that Ashley and I are going to be the next tragic story about two kids finding a gun in the house.

"What did Gramps have to say?" Dad asks, entering the kitchen. "He told me to give that to you."

I fold the clipping and letter and shove them in my pocket. "He's just looking forward to seeing me."

Gramps wants me to unlock his gun safe and break Mom and Dad's trust for a bear swear. Do I really want to go through with this? Just so I can go hunting and maybe see a grizzly? I mean, dragons and vampires are only in stories, but grizzlies are actual living monsters. They can weigh over one *thousand* pounds. They bury horses and eat rotting flesh, and just the thought has my pulse racing. I mean, it's cool and all, but would I be able to outrun a bear? Would Gramps?

I just have so many things on my mind that when Ms. Hoole hands back my test on Monday with a grade of thirty-six and a "See me after class" note, I'm all whatever about it.

When the bell rings and everyone leaves the classroom, I go to her desk and put my test in front of her. "What's up, Hoolio?"

"Tyson," she says, "I'd like to ask you the same question."

"Oh. Yeah. I didn't do so good, did I?"

"Have a seat. I'll write you a pass."

I grab the top chair from a stack in the corner, beneath a map of colonial America, and set it beside her.

"Look here." She points to my name written in her laptop and scrolls across my numbers. "A sixty-one percent on your midterm report, a fifty-five percent on your Jamestown presentation — you didn't even know where Jamestown was. A six*teen* on the Native American tribe quiz."

"So?"

"Tyson, you're failing. If you don't get at least a B minus from here on out, you'll have to repeat this class. I don't want to fail you. You're a very nice kid, and I like you a lot."

"Ms. Hoole, I'm flattered and . . . and I don't know what to think . . . but aren't you married?"

She rolls her eyes. "I'm going to write you a makeup." She hands the test back.

"When is it?"

"Monday. So you'll have a week to study the material again. Maybe you could actually put in some effort this time."

I give her a smile like it's all some big joke, because I'm the kid who can laugh off anything. The thing is, I *did* put in effort. I read the chapter four times, but I just can't remember anything.

"Effort?" I fake a really convincing laugh. I'm a very good actor, and Ms. Hoole has no idea how much her comment hurts. "I wouldn't hold your breath."

I grab my things and leave the classroom.

"What was that about?"

I jerk back. Bright stands outside the door, both hands around his backpack straps.

I say, "Oh, you know. Ms. Hoole wanted me to stay after for 'extra credit,' if you know what I mean." I laugh, but Bright makes no reaction. "How was Steamboat Springs?"

"It was awesome. The guys on the team are really cool."

"I bet."

"You know, we haven't talked about Halloween yet. Wanna walk with me to class?"

"Sure," I say, even though my pre-algebra class is in the

other direction. "I saw these really nasty bear costumes at the mall."

"Um, I'm gonna pass. I think me and some of the guys are going as zombies."

I lower my eyebrows. "Then why'd you ask?"

"I wanted to let you know."

"Because you want to rub it in?"

"We dress up every year, and I know it's important to you."

"Yo, B-Right-On!" Nico shouts out, going the other direction. They bump fists as we pass.

I say, "It's not important to me. I don't care."

"Good."

"I mean, those sound like pretty boring costumes."

"I think they'll be good."

"No, you don't."

"Bright Man!" Gideon, the team's quarterback, and Bright do this handshake in the middle of hallway traffic that takes five seconds to complete.

"What does that mean?" I say.

"It's an inside joke."

I hate it when people say that, because I'm always on the outside.

I say, "*You're* an inside joke."

"What?"

"You think you're hot stuff, but you go on the field for ten seconds and kick a ball. Wow. That's impressive."

I look over. He's shaking his head with this irritating smirk. "You're just jealous."

"Yeah? Well, you're just the kicker. And you lost the game."

He shoves me so hard that I tumble through the traffic and slam against a locker. I want to pummel his face in, but he vanishes into the crowd. Kids point and laugh at me.

I carry on with the rest of my day with my head hung low. By eighth-period homeroom, everyone is saying that Brighton beat me up. I tell them what really happened, but no one believes me.

I hate everything about school.

Monday and Tuesday night come and go, and I don't get any studying in. I'm too busy trying to beat my high score in Great American Hunter 5, and I've killed more elk with head shots than ever before. I even got one from five hundred yards. Wednesday, I eat way too much cereal and nap for like a thousand hours, so no studying then. I have until next Monday — I can study over the weekend. Maybe while me and Gramps are driving to the Tetons.

This trip can't come soon enough. I need to get away from school and never come back.

It would be so awesome to be in the wilderness. I'll live off of grubs and berries and howl at the moon with the coyotes. When winter comes I'll have a shelter made of sticks and mud, a campfire to keep me warm, and a guitar to pass the time. There won't be anyone around for a hundred miles.

When I get home from school on Friday, I go into Gramps's bedroom, find the key, and unlock the gun safe in his closet. The Browning rifles we use at the shooting range are hung up, and boxes of ammunition sit on the top shelf. I stuff it all beneath the clothes in my duffel bag.

The staircase creaks. I zip my bag shut and lock the safe before Dad walks in.

"You know you're not allowed in here," he says suspiciously.

"Gramps wanted me to bring a few of his things." I do a quick search through his closet and grab whatever I can find. The Jenga box.

"Jenga?"

"He wanted to play. What are you doing home so early?"

"I took the afternoon off. I got us reservations for the Red Robin in Rock Springs tonight."

"Ooh, baller status."

"You all ready to go?"

I know he's asking me if I'm done packing. But all I'm thinking is, Am I ready mentally and physically? I've never hunted in my life, I'm going to be out in the wilderness with a man who could be dying, and there will be bears. *Angry* bears.

This is exactly what I need.

"Tyson. You ready?"

I say, "You have no idea."

· CHAPTER 8 ·

The Sunrise Village Nursing Home

I only need two words to describe our trip to Rock Springs: "sagebrush" and "nothing." When we enter Wyoming, there are all these really creepy and secretive military installations with high fences, like they're experimenting on humans or building top-secret predator drones.

I haven't been able to put down Gramps's grizzly book since I read that article he sent me. I need to know my enemy before I enter his territory.

Unlike black bears, grizzlies are incapable of climbing trees to escape a posed threat. Instead, they respond with aggression, standing their ground to ward off potential attackers. This trait also ensures the survival of their cubs. Seventy percent of fatal attacks on humans are caused by a mother grizzly defending her cubs.

That girl from Oklahoma probably just found some bear cubs and thought, *Oh, cute. I'mma go frolic with them!* And then boom, bear paw to the face.

Dad's driving. He puts on his favorite eighties station and the words "Eye of the Tiger" appear on the navigation screen.

He goes, "Can anyone guess what movie this is from? Tyson?"

I look up from my book. "I have no idea."

"Anyone else?"

Mom and Ashley stay quiet.

"*Rocky Three.* Haven't I ever shown you the Rocky movies before?"

I go, "Yeah."

"About the boxer? With Sylvester Stallone? I'm sure you've seen it."

"Oh, yeah."

"Hey, Tyson?"

"Yeah?"

"Did I ever tell you how you got your name?"

About a million times, but he loves telling this story, so I play along.

"Uh . . . Tyson chicken?"

"*Mike* Tyson."

"The guy with the tattoo on his face?"

"Former heavyweight champion of the world. He was known for his unpredictability. One time he took a bite out of Evander Holyfield's ear."

"That's cool."

"When you were born, I was holding you up to my shoulder and you bit my ear. Well, you gummed it, at least. Oh, man, it was so funny. A little Mike Tyson."

"But Dad, I'm a lover, not a fighter."

Mom snickers.

Rock Springs, Wyoming, is this typical suburban-looking city that sits pointlessly in the middle of sagebrush and nothing. Why people decided to settle here, I don't know. Why didn't they settle in the sagebrush ten miles north or south of here? What made this sagebrush better than that sagebrush?

The Sunrise Village Nursing Home is just one hotel-shaped building, three stories tall, with a maze of sidewalks winding through empty flower beds, brown grass, and benches. It's warmer out, and with all the snow melting, it feels more like spring than fall.

Dad pulls into a parking space next to Gramps's pickup, which looks out of place next to all the new and clean cars. I go to the back of the SUV, waiting for him to pop the hatch. But after everyone gets out, he hits the button on his key fob and the horn honks twice.

"Dad." I wiggle the handle on the hatch. "My duffel bag."

"We're not staying here. We got a couple of rooms at the Hampton Inn."

"Oh."

Now how am I going to get Gramps's hunting stuff?

The wide glass doors slide open when I press the big button with a handicap symbol on it.

"Hello, how can I help you?" The receptionist lady's head peeks over the fake granite countertop. Everything in this lobby is cheap. The plants are plastic. The chandeliers, which flicker like candles, are just flame-shaped lightbulbs.

Dad says, "We're here to see my father. His name is Gene."

"He's in room two forty-one. Take a left when you get off the elevator."

We pass an open room with tables and a wall of windows. The more alert old people are playing cards quietly together or talking to visitors. But then there's this one really old lady and she doesn't have any color in her face. She's in her wheelchair facing the window, wearing a bib that's covered in brown snot. Her hands are strapped to the armrests. Her head is bent back like her neck is broken. No one is paying any attention to her.

I knew nursing homes could be bad, but I wasn't expecting this.

"Come on, Tyson." Dad places his hand on my back and guides me to the elevator.

The elevator dings and opens up for us on the second floor.

A stench of pee and cleaning supplies hits me. There's a lady vacuuming who doesn't seem to notice or care that there's this old guy attached to an IV unit standing there, not talking, not doing anything. He has a big wet spot on the crotch of his jeans.

Dad was telling me on the ride up that this is a "state-run" nursing home. He said it isn't going to be as pleasant as some of the other places they checked out, but it's what we can afford. I just . . . Does Gramps really belong in a place like this?

"Gross," Ashley whispers, pinching her nose as we walk past the old man.

I punch her good in the shoulder.

She shoves me back. "Ow. You jerk."

"Show some respect, won't you?"

"Hey, you two," Dad whispers. "Cut it out."

We arrive at room 241. The numbers are polished, but the gold veneer is chipping. Just minutes ago I was all about seeing Gramps. Now I'm terrified to find out what lies beyond this door.

Dad knocks. "Dad? You in there?"

No response.

Dad opens the door and says, drawing the words out, "I brought visitors."

Mom, Dad, and Ashley go in, but I can't and I don't know why.

I peek inside. The room is small — like an economy-size hotel room — and drab from the sunlight coming through the gray curtains. There's a flower-print sofa and a boxy TV atop a stand. There's a little round table with two chairs.

My family goes into the adjoining room and Dad says, "There you are."

"Hi, Gramps," Ashley says, like he's some sick man in a hospital bed.

Mom looks at me with an encouraging smile. "Come on."

No. My feet are like cinder blocks. I can't move. I've wanted to see Gramps all week, but not in this place.

She takes me by the hand.

Gramps is sitting on his perfectly made bed and looking out the window. He has on his red-and-black flannel shirt, his shiny black shoes, and his favorite Henry Feed and Tractor Supply hat. He doesn't look horrible, but he's definitely skinnier.

On his nightstand, there's a faded picture of him and Grandma at their wedding reception. His hair is jet-black and she already has her poofy grandma 'fro. They look so happy together. And it's just the strangest feeling seeing this picture here instead of in the living room by his reclining chair.

Everything is out of place.

"Go on, Tyson," Mom says.

I can't say how I feel with an audience here.

I sit by him and say, "I brought Jenga."

He looks at me.

"It — it's in the car, but Ashley can go get it."

A smile finally crosses his lips, and he pats me on the knee. "It's good to see you, kid."

I throw my arms around him and squeeze him tight. I breathe in the Old Spice.

"We made reservations at Red Robin," Dad says. "We should get moving."

With my arm still around his shoulder, Gramps replies, "I'm not very hungry. We had a big lunch in the cafeteria."

"Ooh, what did you have?" Mom says.

"Chicken and dumplings."

"That sounds delicious."

"Have you been following your diet?" Dad asks.

"Yes, Lee, I have."

Diet?

"I'm not hungry, either," I say. "You guys go without us."

Mom checks her watch. "We'll be back in about an hour. Tyson, you call if anything happens."

"We'll be fine," I say.

As soon as they leave, I turn to Gramps and say, "You haven't eaten yet, have you?"

He shakes his head. "I'm only allowed to eat from a strict menu. It's horrible."

"What's that about?"

He draws out a deep sigh and moves to the other room.

On the end table beneath a pull-string lamp is the stuffed elk and my card, standing upright.

"I suppose it's just a part of getting old," he says.

"Did you like my card?"

He takes a seat on the couch and grabs the stuffed elk, drawing his finger across the little bullet hole on his temple. "You're not supposed to shoot an elk in the head."

In Great American Hunter you get double points for head shots. But all I say is "Oh."

He's annoyed or angry. I would be too if I were living in a place like this. I mean, why is he here? He's not like the other residents who get around in wheelchairs or who can't even remember their own name. I mean, seventy-seven's not *that* old.

Gramps says, "You shoot him in the shoulder. Try and get a head shot and you'll be tracking a dying animal for miles."

"Um, I got your letter. All your stuff is in my bag. You want to leave when they get back?"

"There isn't going to be a hunting trip this year."

"But you said in your —"

"In order to pay for the nursing home, I've had to sacrifice a few things."

"Dad said this was a state-run nursing home. Doesn't that mean the government pays for it?"

"Not all of it."

"If money's the only issue, maybe I could help. How much does Brendan charge?"

"Forty-five hundred for the two of us."

"Oh." I had no idea it cost so much just to shoot some animal. "Then let's hunt with someone else. Or we could go it alone. I mean, we don't need a hunting guide."

"That grizzly is acting up."

"You think it's just one bear?"

"Oh, yeah. It's gotta be Sandy. She's been living in Bridger-Teton for over twenty-five years, and she's earned a nasty reputation. Even charged at me one time, scared me half to death."

"The bear's a girl?"

"She's got the meanest face you can imagine."

"I'm sure the odds of running into her are probably like one in a thousand."

"I wouldn't be so sure."

"Whatever. I'm not afraid of a girl bear."

"Well, do you think you could pack out six hundred pounds of elk meat on horseback? By yourself?"

"Don't underestimate me. Besides, I'll have you right by my side."

Gramps rubs his hands together, and his skin creases in a hundred different places. I imagine that if I opened the window, he would rustle in the wind, just like sheets of paper.

"I've never underestimated you. But Tyson, you are greatly overestimating me."

CHAPTER 9

Two Rifles and a Box of Ammunition

I want to hunt. I want to be hiding in the timber, camouflage paint on my face, my rifle resting on a fallen tree. In the crosshairs of my scope, there's a six-point elk grazing in the open. My finger is resting on the trigger. And I get him right between the eyes. I mean, in the shoulder.

Now it's not going to happen. For the rest of my life, I'll just be some wad who plays hunting video games while eating pizza and I'll never have anything interesting to say to Karen. I've seen her profile. She hunts, she loves fishing, she goes hiking and rides horses with her parents. I wouldn't be able to keep up with her.

I'm tired of being the indoor kid. I wish I had muscles like Bright instead of this shapeless baby fat.

And I want Gramps to be proud of me. I'll show him I can get a mean farmer's tan and take a girl out and ride horses. He's the only person in the family who has a sense of adventure. Dad's so weak and always scared of everything, ninety percent of Mom's life is on her computer, and I don't really know what Ashley does, but she's always in her room. I'm not like them. I'm like *him.*

We have to go, guide or no guide. With or without a place to stay.

Mom, Dad, and Ashley come back an hour and a half later. Not even a second passes before Dad fires a stern glare at me, the Jenga box in his hand.

"Can I see you in the hallway?"

He must really hate Jenga.

Outside Gramps's room, he goes, "I'm not going to yell, but I ought to ground you until you turn eighteen and go off to college."

Now's probably not the time to tell him I have no plans to go to college. "What?"

"Two rifles and a box of ammunition. I went to get Jenga and found them in your duffel bag."

Oh, right.

He says, "How did you get into your grandfather's safe?"

I can't rat Gramps out . . . but I also can't come up with a lie on the spot.

"*Tyson.*"

"Yes, sir?"

"One of the rifles in your duffel bag had the safety off."

"But they weren't loaded."

He pinches the bridge of his nose and sighs. He's so disappointed in me, I can feel it. "What were you thinking?"

"I don't know. I was thinking since we're going to be here this weekend, Gramps and I could go to the Tetons. I brought our elk tags."

"No hunting."

"He paid eight hundred bucks apiece for those tags. They can't just go to waste."

Dad takes a deep breath and lowers his voice a little. "I understand how much this upsets you — I truly do — but the answer is no."

"Are *you* going to take me?"

He takes a second to come up with "You know I have to work."

"Dad, you told me we could go."

He shakes his head. "It's simply too dangerous."

"No, it isn't."

"Your grandfather isn't well."

"What's wrong with him? You can tell me if he has cancer. Is it cancer?"

He opens the door, ready to end this conversation. "You're too young to understand this stuff."

"God, give me some credit!"

So we go back into Gramps's cell and act like everything is okay. We play Jenga on the little table by the window — Mom and Ashley take the two chairs and the rest of us stand, waiting for our turns to come around. Ashley is constantly checking her phone. Mom acts like every piece she pulls from the Jenga tower is as important as defusing a bomb. Dad doesn't say a word, and he *always* picks a middle piece.

For a moment I forget we're in a nursing home instead of at a hunting ranch. For a moment, the situation is tolerable.

The tower gets tall and wobbly and there aren't a lot of safe moves left. I search through the remaining pieces. None of them budge. Maybe I could go for that last middle piece.

"The red wire or the green wire," Gramps says. "Pick a piece and lose, already."

He's not angry. He's just being his usual cocky self. I crack a smile when I wiggle the piece free.

He takes my spot and pokes and prods for the one loose

piece that's just not there. The tower wobbles, and then it comes crashing down. But it wasn't his fault.

"Ashley!" I say. I totally caught her kicking the table. "What the heck?"

"Sorry." Her cheeks flush and she slouches back. "It was an accident."

"Why can't you pay attention?"

"I said I'm sorry."

"Tyson," Mom says, "it's just a game."

"Yeah, I know. But I wanted to win."

"Then let's say you won. Will that make you happy?"

"No, it won't. Ashley's just sitting there and she doesn't want to be here at all, and she probably kicked the table just to end it. I know what she's been thinking ever since we got here—when are we going home? When are we going home?"

Ashley slouches back even farther, and tears start welling in her eyes. But she had it coming   she's such a yamhole.

"That's not what I was thinking," she says.

"Tyson. Settle down," Gramps says. He collects the pieces on the floor. I never expected him to side with anyone but me.

"May I please be excused?" Ashley asks, her hand covering her eyes.

"Yes, you may, sweetheart," Mom replies.

"I'll be waiting outside." She races out of the room and slams the door.

While helping Gramps gather all the pieces, Mom says, "Maybe it's best if we called it a night."

And Dad adds, "And maybe it's best if you go outside and apologize to your sister."

"*She* needs to apologize."

Gramps stands up and puts his hands on his hips. "Go outside and tell your sister that you're sorry. Now."

The heck? Is the entire world against me?

I pass the framed collages hanging outside the residents' doors. A man named Clyde Matthews lives in room 238. In one picture he's a baseball player with a tan and a huge smile. In a much more recent photo all that's left is a sad man sitting in a wheelchair with a birthday hat on his head. In room 236 is Dr. Isabel Brown. In an old Polaroid, she's in her twenties, wearing doctor's clothes and handing a baby over to a brand-new mom. Now, hanging from her door is a sign that says:

DANGER

OXYGEN IN USE

NO SMOKING OR OPEN FLAME

Why should I apologize to Ashley? For putting her in her place? For her not caring that Gramps is stuck here? Should I apologize for thinking of other people before myself?

Ashley's sitting on a bench outside, and I walk right past her. I sit with my back against the front tire of Dad's SUV and start picking the weeds growing out of the cracks in the asphalt. I can see her from over here, her head buried in her hands, crying about what her "mean" older brother said. But what does she really have to cry about? She's coming back to the hotel with us, and she'll have all the time in the world to play with her phone and update her profile status with a sad face.

How could she not care? She was more concerned about McNuggets than Gramps last week.

The doors to the SUV unlock.

I hop to my feet. Dad has his arm around Ashley.

In the car, she refuses to look at me. She's as close to her door as possible, like I've got raging pinkeye.

The radio is playing a dance song from the eighties, about a girl who works hard for the money, so I'd better treat her right.

We're hauling our luggage toward our room, and every

bit of my brain is telling me not to cave in. She doesn't deserve to be treated right, not after the way she's been acting.

"Ashley."

Her cheeks are red, and there's snot under her nose. All she gives me is silence and her sad eyes.

Ashley and I used to hang out all the time. We'd go to Gramps's house after school on the days Mom and Dad both worked, and play Mario Kart. Even though she could never beat me, she'd always be down for a rematch. If I wanted to sled or watch *The Dark Knight* for the fiftieth time, she would, too, even though she hates the Batman movies. Now she just checks her phone, pretending like she's got friends. But I've seen her messages. She texts herself.

Maybe Ashley's not all that bad. Maybe she's just an awkward kid who accidentally kicked the Jenga table.

"I'm sorry," I say.

I don't even know if I mean it, but her doofy smile makes me feel better. It produces *my* doofy smile.

But she's still a yamhole.

CHAPTER 10

Gut Punch

The next day on the way to Sunrise Village, Dad announces that we're heading back home this morning, claiming that Gramps needs to rest. When we arrive at Sunrise, a woman is pushing a little old lady in a wheelchair. I press the handicap button for them.

"Thank you very much," the old lady says. Her smile is brilliant white, like she uses the denture polish of the gods.

"You're welcome, m'lady."

"Oh, I bet you're a Prince Charming with the girls." Her voice rattles, as if she's on a vibrating massage chair.

"Yeah, I get my share."

In the lobby, Dad says, "Your mother and I need to talk to your grandfather, so you two wait out here."

I take a seat in the window room, and Ashley sits three tables away.

"Is this seat taken?" It's the old lady in the wheelchair. She looks like an antique photo come to life. She has on this soft pink dress with white trim that looks like pipe cleaners, and her skinny hands and decrepit arms are covered with battle scars, probably from a life of baking.

I push a chair aside so she can scooch in. "No, go right ahead. What's your name?"

"Marjorie Henry. I'm ninety years young, and you ain't never had a slice of pumpkin pie like *my* pumpkin pie."

She's cute.

I say, "What room are you in?"

"Room two thirty-nine."

"No fooling? My gramps is in two forty-one."

Her eyes widen and her lips purse. "Is his name Gene?"

"He's my gramps."

"I can see where you get your looks. He's got such nice brawny muscles, too. And that full head of silver hair! He looks just like Sean Connery. I always liked men who are good at fixing things."

Ashley peeks over and I can tell she's jealous of me.

I say to Marjorie, "He worked for a feed and tractor

supply place for over thirty years. He can fix anything, from a tractor to a toilet."

"Goodness gracious, he *is* a stud!"

"You should stop in and visit him."

She grabs a pen and a pad of paper from the flower-print purse on her lap. "Here's my number."

Down the hallway the elevator dings, and Mom, Dad, and Gramps get out.

"I guess we should get going," I say to Marjorie.

"I never got your name, young man."

"My name's Tyson."

"Will I see that beautiful smile of yours again, Tyler?"

"It's Tyson. And you bet your lucky bingo cards you will."

Gramps says to me, "Who was that?"

"Her name's Marjorie. I got you her phone number."

"Why'd you do that?"

"Maybe you two could hang out."

He grumbles. "Sometimes I don't know about you."

"What? I'm just saying I think you two would get along. And, you know, you'd have a friend in this place."

Gramps looks at Mom and Dad. "All right if I speak with the boy outside?"

Dad nods.

"Let's go out the back way," Gramps says to me.

I press the blue handicap button. He walks slowly, so I have to press it a second time. He's got something sad on his mind, something I don't want to hear.

They have a pond that backs up to a wire fence, and the highway traffic races by on the other side. A semi farts exhaust, and a puff of black smoke lingers. But the ducks and the old folks don't seem to care.

We take a seat on a bench. Gramps reaches into the breast pocket of his flannel shirt and tosses a chunk of toast toward the shore.

A couple of ducks quack and waddle over.

"We — your parents and I — haven't been entirely honest."

A duck quacks.

Another semi farts.

"No kidding. You told me you didn't like feeding ducks."

A smile crosses his lips, and for a second I imagine what Gramps looked like when he was my age. Dad always says how much we look alike.

He says, "Tyson, my kidneys are shot."

"What does that mean?"

"I've had high blood pressure over half my life, and I suppose it's done a number on them. Rock Springs is the closest place to home that has a dialysis treatment center."

"What's dialysis?"

"Kidneys filter out all the crap from your blood, then you pee it out. They also balance out your electrolytes. Mine don't do that. A dialysis machine pumps the blood from my body, cleans it up, and puts it back in. I have to do it three times a week."

"That sounds horrible."

He rolls up his cuff to reveal stitches and purple bruises on his forearm. "The dialysis needles are too large for my veins, so the doctors had to graft an artery from a cow's neck into my arm."

All of a sudden I'm imagining what my insides look like and all the blood pumping through my veins . . . and then through a cow artery.

"You're kidding."

"That's pure bovine right there. I have to be on a strict diet or else I get sick. That's why your father was so upset when we pruned. Prune juice has too much potassium."

"So?"

"Potassium is an electrolyte."

"What do you have to do to get a new kidney?"

"Someone has to die suddenly, like in a car accident. The

doctors harvest the organs and give them to people on a waiting list. Plus, you have to be a match."

"You're on the list, right?"

He shakes his head. "They don't hand out kidneys to old-timers."

"But y — you know, you fought in Korea and you have a Purple Heart and saved lives."

He nods, and it's like a gut punch. Gramps has been thrown away. That's why he's here.

I'm fighting back tears of pure rage. He doesn't deserve to be treated like this, not after all he's done. He's my friend. He's family. How can he go out like this, just because of a couple of stupid kidneys?

Then it occurs to me.

"Wait," I say. "You can take a kidney from someone in your family. Take one of mine! I'm not using both of them." I recall my human anatomy from biology class. "Kidneys are like livers, right? We all have two."

"You only have one liver."

"Really?"

"It's a nice thought, but I can't take one of your kidneys."

"Come on, let's go into surgery today."

"My body physically can't accept your kidney."

"I might not have muscular man kidneys yet. But mine work really well."

"How many Pixie Stix have you had this morning?"

"Come on, Gramps. We'll be kidney brothers."

Gramps groans his way out of his seat, returning the way we came — toward the sidewalk that winds to the glass doors, the nursing home, and a life that doesn't include me.

"Tyson," he says, his back to me, "I'm not your real grandfather."

CHAPTER 11

I Call Gramps by His First Name

My brain is frozen like my five-year-old laptop and I can't get it to reboot. Not my real grandfather? What does that even *mean*?

I finally execute my internal Control+Alt+Delete command, sending a message to my legs to move. But Gramps has already gone inside, and it's just Mom, Dad, and Ashley together on the hallway bench.

"Where'd he go?"

Dad says, "He's getting ready for his dialysis."

"Is something wrong, honey?" Mom says. "You look upset."

"Oh, yeah, you know. Gramps just told me he's not my real grandfather."

"Yes, he is," Dad says defensively. He's lying to my face, and I can't even look at him.

Mom brushes my cheek with the back of her hand, and I smack it away. Her eyes well with tears. But why? Because she thinks I'm a little boy who needs his mommy?

I'm so angry at her. I'm so angry at everyone.

She says, "I know this must be a lot for you."

My skull is just burning with anger. She *knows* it must be a lot for me? She thinks she knows what's going on in my head?

I say, "Okay. Listen, Mother. You don't talk this way to Dad; you don't even talk this way to Ashley. Why do you have to treat me like this? Do you guys think I'm stupid?"

"No, honey, we don't —"

"Stop calling me 'honey' or 'sweetie' or 'baby.' I'm *thirteen*."

"Then what do you want?" she asks.

This feels like a prank. Why couldn't they have just told me? I'm fully capable of knowing that Gramps isn't my real grandfather without it destroying me. They lied to me for thirteen years!

I say, "Let's just go home."

It hurts. I mean *really* hurts. Everyone thinks I'm an idiot. It's hard to breathe, as if bee stings are swelling my throat shut.

We're driving through this pointless city that's got nothing but a Red Robin, a nursing home, and a dialysis center, and then we get back on the highway. My book is in my lap. I can't stop staring out the window. My jaw hurts from clenching my teeth.

I say, "What's his real name?"

Mom looks up from her novel, pretending she doesn't know what I'm talking about. "I'm sorry?"

"Gene," I say. "What's his last name?"

"It's Driggs," Dad says flatly. "I adopted his last name when he and your grandmother got married."

"So what happened to my real grandfather?"

Dad pauses. It seems like he's going to say something but changes his mind.

Mom leans over the seat. "Your father doesn't like talking about him."

"Connie, please," he gripes, and motions her to turn around.

It gets quiet again, except for the boops and beeps from Ashley's headphones. I take out one of her earbuds and say, "Did you know about this?"

"About Gramps?"

"Yeah."

She nods.

Oh, my God, they told *Ashley*? They think *Ashley* is more mature than me? She's the most childish girl ever! My face is getting hot and teary, and I've got to get out of this car. Everyone thinks I'm a baby, like I need special treatment. Even Gramps. Or Gene. Whatever.

I want to scream, but I bite it down. If I scream, that'll just prove their point. I won't say anything for the rest of the trip. I'm just gonna sit here.

When we cross over the border back into Colorado, Dad says, "Tyson, I got a phone call from your American Civilization teacher yesterday. She said you need to get your grade up. I understand you have a makeup test on Monday."

Don't say anything.

"She says you need to get a B to pass her class. We'll come back here next weekend, but only if you get a B. Tyson, did you hear me?"

Say something. If I don't answer, he'll think I'm being immature.

I say, "I heard you went hunting when you were my age."

"Who told you that?"

"Gene." Whoa, it feels weird calling him by his first name. But everyone needs to know that I can handle whatever. Give me any bad news, and I'll take it like a champ.

"You're calling him Gene?" Dad says.

"What should I call him?"

"I don't even call him Gene. It sounds weird coming out of your mouth."

"He's not my grandfather and, you know, I'm fine with that. But I'm not going to call him something he isn't." Then I say, "So Gene told me you didn't field-dress your elk."

"What's your point?" he says with an edge.

"I could do it."

"Talk to me again when you've got a five-hundred-pound animal lying in front of you."

"So can we still go?"

Mom shakes her head. "No, no, no. I don't want you going."

"But it's the last weekend before the season ends."

"I don't want either of you getting eaten. One guy lost his arm."

"You're overreacting to one little bear story." I'm banking on Mom having missed the article about the sixteen-year-old girl.

Dad says, "Do you even know how to ride a horse? You know everything has to be done on horseback out there — they don't allow vehicles."

"Whatever. We rode horses during our fifth-grade camping trip."

"Have you already forgotten where we just came from? Your grandfather is in a *nursing* home."

"Well, yeah, but he's not, like, *super* old. He just needs dialysis. Everything else about him is fine."

"A sick old man and a kid who hasn't hunted a day in his life going into the wilderness? All by themselves? That sounds like a smart idea."

"What if we found another guide?"

"Do you understand what your grandfather's going through?"

"I also understand that you promised me we'd go. Remember my birthday?"

Every year, Mom and Dad get me a bunch of small presents and one big present. They didn't have money to get me anything except for some new school clothes this year, so they said my big present would be the elk hunt.

"Things have changed," he says.

"So you're breaking your promise."

"Tyson . . ."

"No, just say it. You told me that we could go hunting, and now you're saying we can't."

"Enough! This conversation is over."

It doesn't matter that Gene isn't family or that his kidneys don't work. And it doesn't matter what Dad says or how loud he says it. I still want to be able to hang with Karen. I still want to get in better shape. I still want to know what it means to be a hunter. And I *need* to show everyone that I'm a man, because I'm tired of being treated like a kid.

Despite my best intentions to study when we get back home, I google other hunting guides instead. They all charge way more than Brendan Rien.

And then I google Taylor Swift.

Then I google dialysis. One page leads to another, and I end up at a site that talks about these machines you can have at home that do all the same things the ones at a clinic do.

Gene moving three hours away isn't his only option. He could still live at home. Why didn't anyone else think of this?

I probably should exercise and get in shape for the trip.

I do twelve push-ups until my arms are on fire and I fall face-first on the carpet. Then I do about ten sit-ups and the burning feeling in my stomach sucks, so I turn on Great American Hunter 5.

Dad opens my door. Without knocking, of course. He's holding the house phone. "It's for you."

"Who is it?"

"Brighton."

My heart races a little. I haven't talked to him since he shoved me against a locker.

Dad looks at the TV and says, "This game is so horrible. Going around shooting animals like a . . . like a barrel of monkeys."

"Huh?"

"Turn it off. You need to be studying for your makeup test."

I take the phone, then shoo Dad away. "Hey, what's up?"

"Hey, Tyson," Bright says. "I tried messaging you on your phone."

"Battery's dead." But the truth is, I just didn't want to talk to him.

"I'm, uh—things have been good. I was just, uh, seeing what you were up to tonight." Bright clears his throat with a cough. "And, you know, to see how you've been doing. Haven't talked to you in a while."

"You want to hang out? You're not partying with the ladies?"

"Heh, no."

"What about Nico and Timmy?"

"I don't know. I kinda just want to hang with you."

My chest inflates. Maybe Brighton's coming to his senses and remembering that we're best friends and that's not a title you just throw away.

I should stop doubting myself. I'm cooler than Mika or the football kids. Who else would sing karaoke with him? Not Nico or Timmy. They take themselves too seriously. Who else would play Mario Kart with him for six hours? Definitely not Mika. She'd be bored after three.

But can we still be friends after what happened?

"Are you serious?" I say.

"You have the latest Great American Hunter, right?"

"It's so much fun."

"Bring it over. And if you haven't had dinner, I ordered pizza."

"Party."

Maybe I can get the old Brighton back. Well, more like the *younger* Brighton. Before he started football conditioning. Before he started texting Mika every fifteen minutes. Before he buzzed off his hair and put on body spray and got an attitude.

I hurry downstairs. "Mom, can you give me a ride to Brighton's? I'm going to spend the night."

Dad comes out of the kitchen with a bowl of popcorn. It's Saturday night, which is movie night for my folks.

"You have to study for your makeup test," he says.

Oh, right.

I come up with "That's what we're doing. Bright got an A on our last test and he said he'd help me."

Dad sits next to Mom on the couch. She lays her legs across his lap and takes a handful of popcorn. She has this smirk on her face, like she knows better.

So it surprises me when she says, "You got your things?"

"In my backpack."

Mom gets up and hunts for her coat in the hallway closet. The whole time, Dad is looking at me, then at her. He chews his popcorn really slow, like he's totally confused. I kinda am, too. There's no way she's falling for this.

"You ready?" she says from the front door.

"Uh . . . yeah?"

So we get in her minivan and like always, she keeps the radio off. She pulls out of the driveway and doesn't say a word until we reach the first stoplight. It's kind of unsettling, so I hug my backpack.

Finally, she says, "Tyson, your real grandfather wasn't . . . very nice with your grandmother and your dad. He doesn't like talking about him."

"What did he do?"

"Your father won't even tell me."

"Really?"

"He died a year before you were born, and your dad didn't even go to the funeral. When your dad and I first started dating, he talked about Gene like he was a superhero. He went on and on about their adventures growing up. Gene had this beautiful Chevy Impala and during the summers they traveled all around the country. Your grandfather, or Gene, or whatever you want to call him, they don't make them like him anymore."

"Yeah," I say. "He is pretty cool." But I really hope Mom's done with this conversation. It just hurts thinking about anything Gramps-related. I mean Gene-related.

Mom pats my leg. "Now, look, I know you and Bright aren't studying tonight, but —"

"What? Yes, we are."

"Can I see what's in your backpack?"

I hold it tighter to my chest. There isn't anything in there but a video game and a box of Fruit Roll-Ups.

She says, "Have fun tonight, but promise me that tomorrow you *will* study for your test."

"I bear swear."

"Huh?"

So at the last stop sign before Brighton's house, I show her how to make her hands into claws. We interlock them and I growl.

"Bear swear," she says, and laughs a little. "I like that."

"Ain't it great?"

She pulls up to Brighton's driveway. I get out and close the door. And inside my head, I thank her for being somewhat awesome.

CHAPTER 12

She Wears Short Skirts;
I Wear Pizza

I ring the doorbell and Bright answers with Chloe by his side like some confused and nugget-shaped body-guard. We're both wearing our Bubba Gump Shrimp Company shirts that we got when he joined us on our California trip two summers ago. His shirt is too small, but mine still fits me fine.

"Nice shirt," he says. "Want some pizza?"

"Well, you know, I am a hungry bear." I smile.

He nods, unimpressed, and closes the door. Hungry bear? Guh, I'm so stupid.

Beneath the hallway chandelier, I see something on the bridge of his nose — a zit that has been covered with a layer of concealer. It's cracked, and the color doesn't match his skin. I pretend not to notice.

We go into the living room. There's a sound of kids laughing and an air-hockey puck clacking against mallets coming from the basement.

"Is someone else here?" I say. I thought it was just going to be us tonight.

"Oh, uh, yeah. I invited over a couple of friends."

"Who?"

Downstairs in Bright's Hang Zone, Timmy and Nico are playing air hockey. They look like high-schoolers. Mika is watching them play, and . . .

Oh, my God. Karen's here. Her palms are against the table and her hair's down and she's so . . . hot.

Timmy and Nico stop playing and they all look at me. Their smiles make me uneasy, and something about this doesn't feel right.

"What's up, Ty?" Nico says. "You two look like twinsies. Did you guys, like, plan that out?"

"No," Bright and I say.

"This is Karen," Mika says.

"Hey, I'm Karen." She gives me a little wave. Her voice sounds more mature than I imagined.

"Karen just moved here from Texas," Mika says. "She sits next to me in English."

"Oh, Texas?" I say, my throat in a knot. After an

awkward silence, I blurt, "So, Karen, do you like beards?"

Now I officially hate myself.

"No?"

"I thought everyone in Texas wears beards."

Everyone busts up laughing. They're laughing *at* me. And Bright just stands there, not helping at all.

Karen says, "Mika tells me you're going elk hunting with your grandpa."

Oh, man, I love her Texas twang.

"Uh-huh" is all I can manage. I must look like the biggest idiot.

"I hunt with my brothers at our uncle's ranch. I've shot wild boars, whitetail deer . . . One time I went to this place, Five-J Hunting Ranch. They keep exotics there, and I shot myself a scimitar-horned oryx."

"Yeah, I know."

She cocks her head back. "How'd you know?"

Oh, crap. I gotta think of an excuse.

Timmy says, "Because he checks your status every day. Total stalker." He puts the puck on the table with the most infuriating smile. "Five to three."

My skin gets cold. Did Brighton tell him? He's the only

one who knows I have a crush on Karen, and he promised to keep it secret.

"Really?" Karen says.

"Shut up, Timmy. I do not."

"That's not what Bright said."

Bright stands there, sipping a can of Dr Pepper, acting like he didn't do anything wrong. Why am I a topic of discussion with his new group? What else do they know?

This is why I'm here. He brought me over to embarrass me, not in front of his new friends but in front of Karen.

"You know, I should get going," I finally say. "I got to study for Ms. Hoole."

"You're leaving?" Nico says. "You got here like two minutes ago."

"I just came over to say hello. My mom's waiting out front."

Bright follows me up the staircase and closes the basement door behind him. I march to the front door.

"Tyson."

"Thanks for punking me."

"Dude, I'm sorry. Timmy shouldn't have said that. He's such a butthead."

"*You're* the butthead." Guh, my eyes are getting all wet,

but I refuse to cry just because Brighton sucks now. With my back turned I say, "Is this what you guys do all day? Sit around and make fun of me?"

"Dude, it's not like that."

"Why did you tell them about Karen? Now she thinks I'm a psycho."

"I don't know. We were at the field after practice and we were just talking. And they asked about you."

"Because they think I'm a joke."

"It's not that."

"I'm not an idiot."

"Dude, okay, you wore a Taylor Swift T-shirt last week to school. You bought tickets to her concert the day they went on sale. I mean, come on. You were asking for it."

"What? You don't like her? Did we not sing 'Mean' at Party Fiesta Karaoke for your birthday?"

"Well, yeah, but I don't go broadcasting it," he says, almost whispering.

"What's so wrong about liking Taylor Swift?"

"Are you serious? We're in eighth grade. Next year we'll be in high school. Only girls like Taylor Swift." He points at my belt and says, "And that rattlesnake belt buckle is just the ugliest thing."

Okay, don't punch him in the gonads. He knows Gene got me that belt last Christmas. And I mean, yeah, the buckle is practically the size of a salad plate, but it means a lot to me.

I say, "So did you tell them all my secrets?"

"Not *all* your secrets. But these guys have known each other since last year, and I had nothing to say. And they wanted to know everything about you. I didn't mean to throw you under the bus — honest — but they just wouldn't stop asking. It was Timmy's plan to bring you over here and do this."

"You're such a butt. How would you feel if I told them all your secrets? Like the time you wet the bed in the fourth grade. Or I'll tell them you have all the *Gossip Girl* episodes on your computer."

His eyes sharpen. "Dude. Don't."

"And it's so obvious you put makeup over that zit."

Bright immediately faces the floor, his face shadowed. In a small voice, he says, "It's tinted acne cream."

I open the front door. "Thanks for ruining my only chance with Karen."

With his hand covering his nose, he says, "You know, you wouldn't have even talked to her if it weren't for us."

"Yeah-huh."

"You're too scared to talk to girls."

I close the door. But then I open it again and *slam* it.

That's so not true. I'd planned this for weeks—I was going to talk to Karen after I went hunting, because I wanted to have something interesting to say to her. Instead, I blathered on about beards.

I walk. It ain't bad—maybe two miles, all on lit roads with little traffic. We live in a pretty nice town and I don't know of any creepers. No sketchy white vans. It just sucks how quickly the temperature drops when the sun goes down.

My phone moos. A call from Bright. I hit IGNORE.

That's it. I'm asking Karen out, and I don't care if she turns me down or laughs in my face. I have to do this.

When I get home forty-five minutes later, I go into the living room and the TV's on—a Country Music Channel presentation on Taylor Swift. Ashley's asleep on the couch with her hands tucked beneath her head. She looks cute, like a little kid all tuckered out after some intense frolicking.

It still smells like popcorn in here, but like always, Mom and Dad went to bed way before the movie ended.

I sit in Gramps's reclining chair and turn the volume

up. They're talking about the making of the video for "You Belong with Me." I haven't seen this one yet.

Ashley looks up, her hair messy. "Hey."

"Yo."

"Dad said you were spending the night at Brighton's."

"Change of plans."

She looks at the TV and then back at me, confused. "You can change the channel if you want."

"Are you kidding? I love Taylor Swift."

"Really?"

Ashley and I don't talk often. Come to think of it, we don't talk to each other at all anymore.

"Yeah," I say. "She's a musical genius."

"Now you're messing with me."

Bright might be embarrassed by the things he likes, but I refuse to be ashamed of loving Taylor Swift. She writes all her own music, her first album came out when she was only sixteen, her songs are super catchy . . . and she's hot.

My phone beeps. A message from Bright, or, as he's saved in my phone, *B-Right-On.* That was my nickname for him. I thought of it in the first grade. Now everyone uses it, so I don't anymore.

I put my phone back in my pocket. "I know everything

about her," I say. "Did you know she did magazine ads telling girls to drink low-fat milk?"

"Of course I know that. Wow, but I can't believe *you* know that."

"Yeah, well, I tend to surprise people."

She sits up a little. "Did you know she won a national poetry contest when she was a kid?"

I roll my eyes. "It was called 'Monster in My Closet,' and she won the contest when she was in the fourth grade. She also wrote a three-hundred-and-fifty-page novel."

"Yeah, right. How come I never heard about it?"

"Isn't it obvious? You're not the Taylor Swift fan that I am."

Her confusion turns into joy. "How come you never told me? Ooh, we could go to the concert in Denver!"

"Tickets already sold out." I don't tell her I have a pair. I was originally supposed to go with Bright — he even asked me to get him a ticket. But I can't go with Ashley. I mean, she's my sister.

She goes, "Well, if I can find tickets, do you want to go?"

"Only if you can keep up with me, 'cause I was planning on going all out. I'm talking face paint, matching shirts, glow sticks . . ."

"Okay, now you're starting to freak me out."

I take the remote and crank the volume. I jump on the couch one cushion away from her and jam out to the bridge of "You Belong With Me" on my air microphone with a death-metal voice.

"Tyson!" she cries out in a whisper. "Mom and Dad are upstairs!"

I do one more hop and collapse, my legs stretched across her lap. I wiggle my feet in front of Ashley's face, and she pushes them away.

"You're gross." But she's laughing so much. This feels like the time to ask her something that's been bugging me since last Friday.

I say, "How come you didn't care when I told you they put Gene in a nursing home?"

"Huh?"

"You were all whatever about it."

"Oh. Um, I don't know."

"You really don't care?"

"I care. I mean, of course. I just . . . don't like to talk about things like that."

"What do you mean?"

"I'm tired of everything being bad all the time. Dad losing his job and getting depressed, and then our living in a motel. We were, like, homeless. All of my stuff is still in boxes. And then when you told me about Gramps . . ." She lets out a long sigh. "I should have seen it coming. But why would I say anything?"

"It would have helped me."

She tucks her knees up to her chest, looking me in the eyes. "I thought you never wanted to talk to me."

"Tell me something about yourself I don't know. What do you like to do?"

"Study," she confesses, like she's ashamed.

"Are you smart?"

"Yeah. I can help you get ready for your test if you want."

"But you're eleven."

"I'm in Advanced American Civ. We studied the Revolutionary War three weeks ago."

"Really? Wow, okay."

She gathers up her things. "I'm going to bed. 'Night."

I steal her spot, cover myself with the blanket, and watch a marathon of Taylor Swift stuff.

Okay, tomorrow I'm going to study my yamhole off. No excuses.

My phone goes off so early, the sun isn't even up. I hear my ringtone.

Moo.

Who the heck is calling me at . . . what time is it? God, it better not be Bright.

Moo. Moo.

My phone isn't in my pants pockets, not on the end table.

"Seriously, Bright, I'm going to kill you."

My phone moos again.

There! I fish it out from between the couch cushions.

It's five a.m. GRAMPS is flashing on my screen.

CHAPTER 13

Someone Karen Would Like

Gene never uses his cell phone for anything other than emergencies. He kept it in the cup holder of his pickup in case of an accident. This call has to be important. And I have a feeling it's about the hunting trip.

"Gene," I say. "Hey."

"So you're calling me Gene now?"

"Um . . . yeah."

There's an awkward moment where I think about what happened yesterday at the nursing home. But I won't bring it up. And I know he won't, either.

He says, "You still coming to see me next weekend?"

"That depends. Dad says I have to pass this test tomorrow."

"Good. I can't have my hunting partner be a middle-school dropout."

"Hunting partner?" I say with fake excitement. I want to go. I really do. But guys on dialysis don't hunt elk. Gene has gotten weaker and skinnier, and I can't have him go on this trip just because I need to prove something. I mean, God, what if something happened out there?

I say, "How is that going to work out?"

"I had dinner with Marjorie Henry last night."

"Oh, yeah? She's cool, isn't she? So did you get a kiss?"

"Always looking out for the important things."

"You know it."

"Tyson, Marjorie is the widow of Martin Henry."

"Your old boss?"

"He owned a ranch in the Bridger-Teton National Forest. It's where we would hunt back in the day. Marjorie owns the ranch now. She said we can use it whenever we want, free of charge."

"That's fun."

"Her nephew Mike runs the place with his girlfriend. They have horses, all-terrain vehicles, and . . ." He gets into a coughing fit.

"Are there going to be hunting guides?"

"No."

"But Dad hid your rifles."

"Mike has a couple set aside for us."

"But Mom won't let me go to the Tetons 'cause of the bear attacks."

"Just tell them that we're going camping someplace, maybe in Idaho. No grizzlies in Idaho."

"You want me to lie?"

"We bear swore that we'd go on this hunt. And you *never* break a bear swear. I don't care what your mother thinks, what your father thinks, what my nurses think, or what anyone thinks. We're going."

What about what I think?

I say, "What about your kidneys? Don't you have to do dialysis three times a week?"

"I have an appointment Friday. We'll leave for the Grand Tetons early the next morning."

I swallow hard. An image appears: Gene getting sick in the middle of the wilderness, and me the only one around to help him.

I feel a heavy weight on my shoulders that makes my bones ache. I've never had to worry about anything other than tests or middle-school drama, but now I'll be in charge of a sick seventy-seven-year-old man in the heart of grizzly bear country.

Am I up to it? Heck, no. But I can't show weakness. I can't say what I truly feel. So I say, "You didn't answer my question. Did you get a kiss?"

There's silence on the other end of the line.

Finally he says, "I got *two* kisses. That old lady is crazy."

What does this trip mean to him? I don't know why, but I think of Grandma. They were one of those perfect couples you only see in movies. They held hands and kissed in public and they were together for years and they never got bored with each other. He called her his angel.

Grandma's been dead for four years, and as much as Gene acts like it doesn't bother him and as tough as he is, he has to be sad. And now his health is gone, and now the people he calls his family live three hours away.

Gene deserves this trip. But does that mean we should go? I have no idea. All I know is I at least want to see him this weekend. He lives a state away, but I won't let that change things between us. We'll be just as tight as always.

I go upstairs and knock on Ashley's door. "Ashley," I whisper. I say her name two more times and get nothing.

So I try "Hey, yamhole."

She opens the door with crazy hair and sleepy eyes. "Yam *what*?"

"It's a word I made up."

"That's stupid."

"Talk to me in a year when everyone's saying it. It'll be in, like, rap songs and kids will be saying 'That's totally yam.'"

She gives me her you're-such-an-idiot eye roll. "What do you want?"

"Come and help me study. I'll make you pancakes."

"It's too early."

"I can only see Gene this weekend if I get a B on my test." She groans. "All right."

I'm feeling good. Even though there's no way Gene's lie will work, I'll still get to see him. And he *is* my best friend. He would never betray me for the cool kids in the nursing home.

I flip up some of the best pancakes ever, 'cause they have my secret ingredient in them — blueberries. With my country music playlist on, I'm stacking 'em up on Ashley's plate.

She turns my phone off. "I want you to write down each question from your last test on these flash cards. And on the other side, write down the answer."

"But Ms. Hoole's not even going to test me on these questions. She's going to make new ones."

"Just do it," she says with a groan.

When Ashley quizzes me, I'm surprised by how many I get right.

I say, "How did I do this?"

"When you have multiple-choice or fill-in-the-blank tests, make flash cards. The way you've been studying, you just skim through the chapter."

Jeez, maybe I could be good at anything. Maybe I could kick a football farther than Bright. Heck, maybe I'm the greatest kisser the world has ever known.

The next morning, I'm able to get in two sets of ten push-ups and fifteen sit-ups, and then I do some arm curls with my backpack loaded with my books. I walk to school eating one of Mom's really dry and disgusting protein bars.

Ms. Hoole is typing on her laptop in homeroom. The test waits on the desk in front of her.

"Hey, Tyson. Have a seat. You'll have fifty minutes to finish, and if you have any questions, feel free to ask."

The first three questions are all ones that Ashley quizzed me on yesterday. This thing is easy. I mean, the Boston Tea Party? More like, the Boston I-Just-Answered-You-Correctly Party.

I hand in my test with ten minutes left.

"Done already?" She takes out her red pen, does her marks, then hands the paper back. And there it is, an eighty-eight written in her bubbly handwriting. Next to a smiley cat face. I'm trying to act all normal, but my brain is tingling and my hands are warm. This is the first time in forever that my grade isn't accompanied by a grumpy cat face.

The bell rings for first period, and I hurry to the auditorium, where Karen sits on the far end. With my test stuffed into my back pocket, I take the chair one row behind her, my closest so far.

Don't be myself. Don't be the psycho Internet stalker she met at Brighton's. Be cool and/or funny and have one of those hot half smiles and slightly narrowed eyes.

I got this.

I poke her neck with my pencil eraser. "Hey."

"Ow." Karen turns. Her eyebrows are furrowed, and she's rubbing her neck. "What was that for?"

"What *wasn't* it for?"

She smirks. I can work with that. She says, "Didn't really get a chance to talk to you the other night. Not too often I meet another hunter."

"Yeah, well, you know. I don't like to brag."

"What kind of animals do you hunt?"

I force back a stutter. "Elk, mostly."

"Oh, yeah, my granddad told me this area has some of the largest elk herds. I see 'em all over the place. What's your largest one?"

"Oh, well, there was this one time last season I shot a buck with six points."

"Bull."

How can she see right through me? "I'm not lying."

"No, no. You said you shot a buck, but bucks are male deer. *Bulls* are male elk."

"Oh, yeah. I shoot so many, sometimes I get confused."

She nods, and I can only pray she believes me. "So you just go out in your backyard and shoot one?"

"We don't hunt the elk here. We go to the Grand Tetons."

"Fun! My granddad says Wyoming's got a lot of regulations. You don't have to prove the animal's sex in Texas."

"That's weird." I have no idea what she's talking about.

"What's it like?"

"Huh?"

"I've never field-dressed an animal. The hunting guides on the ranch always did the dirty work. What's it like cutting open an elk?"

"Like breaking open a piñata, I guess. But instead of candy falling out, there's like . . . intestines."

"Ew!" The sound of her laughter is so rewarding. I have to keep this up. She says, "You gotta show me pictures. Are there any online?"

"We didn't take pictures. But we will this year, I bear swear."

"What's bear swear?"

Just like Gene showed me, and just like how I showed Mom, I have her make her hands into bear claws. Her fingers interlock with mine. Her hands are so soft, and she's got this amazing smile.

Looking her dead in the eyes, I shake our hands violently with a growl. She bursts into a honking laugh. It's so unexpected and dorky.

"I love bears," she says.

"Me, too."

Mr. Cavner enters the room and tells the class to be quiet. Karen turns around and she's choking back a fit of laughter.

Today we sing "I Wanna Be Loved by You."

There's no question about it — I'm getting the bear costume. And the hunting trip is so on.

CHAPTER 14

The Headline Story

I post an ad on Craigslist.

Aquarium and all the stuff for it. 75 dollars.

But that's not going to be enough for the bear costume. I need three hundred. And there's only one valuable thing that I have.

I look at my Taylor Swift tickets. It's a concert that I've wanted to see since fifth grade. But I'm the only guy in my grade who admits to liking her.

I mean, I don't *have* to see her. And besides, the bear costume is so cool. The fur looks like it was skinned from an actual bear, and it's got the meanest face you can imagine. This costume would make a statement — I am strong like bear. I make eating berries and grazing look fierce.

Karen is going to love it.

There's a pile of clean laundry on my bed. I fold my Taylor Swift T, then tuck it into the bottom dresser drawer beneath a stack of shirts that smell like the back rack at Goodwill. And then I post the ad.

Two Taylor Swift tickets for sale. Second row seats. 250 bucks for the pair.

Within minutes, my phone moos.

"Hello?"

"Hi, I'm calling about the Taylor Swift tickets," says some girl.

"Yeah, I'm selling them for two fifty."

"Is there any way you could sell them cheaper?"

"How much cheaper?"

"All I have is two hundred."

"Two *hundred*? These tickets sold out in fifteen minutes."

"I know, but they're for my brother."

Oh, my God, is this Ashley?

She goes, "He said he'd go with me if I got tickets."

It's got to be her. This is too good. I say, "Well, maybe we could make a trade."

"Um . . ."

"Tell you what—two hundred bucks for the pair, but you got to throw in your Nintendo DS Lite."

The other line goes silent. "Tyson?"

Now I'm laughing. "You can pick up your tickets at thirteen fourteen Corona Drive."

"Tyson!"

I hear Ashley scampering down the hall.

With one hand on the knob, she says in the doorway, "You have Taylor Swift tickets? How did you get tickets?"

I wave them at her. "Told you I was a bigger fan."

She goes for them, but I pull away.

I say, "Do we have a deal?"

"Wait, you're not actually going to sell them to me."

"Uh-huh."

She sits down on the bed next to me and says, "The whole reason I wanted to buy these tickets was so we could go together. Now we can."

"Yeah, but I need this money to buy my Halloween costume."

"Why are you spending so much on a costume?"

"'Cause it's awesome. And then me and Gene are going on our trip."

"Tyson!" She jumps to her feet. "There's no way Dad's letting you go."

"Yeah, he will, when I tell him we're going to the Caribou-Targhee National Forest."

"But that's in Idaho."

"Check this place out." I flip open my laptop to their website. "Me and Gene are going fishing, and they have horseback riding and you can even pan for gold. Fun, huh?"

She gives me this knowing stare. "Are you really going to Idaho?"

"That depends. Are you cool?"

"Huh?"

"Are you cool? I mean, are *we* cool?"

"Um, yeah. We're cool."

"It's where Dad *thinks* we're going."

"Tyson, no. You can't go to the Tetons. There's grizzlies up there."

"I know."

"Haven't you seen the news?"

"Whatever. That was, like, a week ago."

"No, no. The couple from Ohio."

"Huh?"

"This couple from Cleveland were in their tent and a grizzly bear knocked it down and killed them."

"What? When?"

"It was all over the news this morning. It happened in the Tetons yesterday."

"Yeah, right. You're just like Mom."

She takes my laptop and shows me the headline story on my home page.

Bear Attack in Bridger-Teton National Forest Kills Two Hunters.

I read the headline over and over, trying to process it. This happened in the exact place Gene and I will be hunting. And all I can picture is Sandy, the fur around her face matted with blood and her belly engorged with human body parts.

I go, "They just meant a bear *attacked* two hun —"

"*Killed,*" Ashley stresses. "You can't go. I don't want you to get hurt."

"I'm going."

"But why?"

"I have to."

"No, you don't."

"Ashley, you don't understand. Even if there were fifty thousand bear attacks this year and I had a ninety percent chance of getting eaten alive, I would still go. Yeah, I'm scared. Of course I'm a little scared, but what would Gene say? He'll probably never get to go hunting again."

"Please, Tyson. Please, please — you can't go."

"There really isn't anything you can say to stop me."

"I could tell Dad that you're lying to him. Think you'd be able to go then?"

"Ashley. Come on, I thought we were cool."

"You don't realize it now, but I *am* being cool."

My phone moos. Another local number that I've never seen before.

"You could tell Dad," I say, "and I could take this call."

"You wouldn't."

I secretly hit IGNORE on my phone and put it up to my ear. "Hello?" I say. "The Swift tickets? Yeah, they're still available."

Ashley opens her wallet. Two bills fall onto my bed. Benjamin Franklin's face is on the front. "I won't tell Mom or Dad. But please, please, please, you have to be safe."

Before Mom gets back from the store and Dad gets home from work, I've found someone to take Jar Jar Newtingston's old home off my hands. She's a cute young mom who just bought her eight-year-old son some guppies.

So it's official — the saga of Pizza Bear and Booger Bear 5000 has come to an end.

I don't want it to hurt, but when she carries the aquarium away, my chest gets that burning sad feeling I've been getting a lot lately. It's like, yeah, Bright's not my friend anymore so it shouldn't be a big deal. But he *was* my friend.

Someday I'll get over it.

When I hear the sound of the garage door rumbling open, I go downstairs to meet Dad at the door leading to the garage. "Hey."

"Tyson. What's happening?"

"Not much. I just rocked Ms. Hoole's face off." I show him my test.

"Hey, nice job, buddy."

"So can you take me to the mall? I need to get my costume."

An hour later, we're walking by empty stores and the broken fountain. I used to toss pennies in there when I was a kid and wish that Mom would buy me a Transformer. This place used to be so packed, but now it's like ancient ruins.

"Hey, Dad? I was looking online the other day, and have you ever heard of home dialysis?"

"The machines cost forty thousand dollars," he says, as if he were prepared for my question. "Plus certified nurses and installation—it's money we simply don't have."

There's got to be a better option than a nursing home in another state. But there aren't any dialysis centers here. There isn't much of anything here. We have Chipotle and the Bargain Barn, and they're talking about putting in a Jamba Juice, but I'm not getting my hopes up.

The costume shop has been cleaned out except for my costume, hanging like a skinned bear and all by itself on the back rack.

When I go to the cashier and he's ringing me up, I see the grand total. And I'm short on money.

The cashier has on a pair of pink bunny ears and painted-on whiskers, a button nose, and a name tag that says KIERNAN. He says dully, "Looks like you're going to have to take it back."

"Here," Dad says to me. "Give me your money, and I'll put it on my card."

"Dad, you don't have to do this."

"I don't know why you want this goofy outfit so bad, but if it means that much to you." He hands the cashier his credit card.

Wow. Maybe it's because of the weather or because I got a B on my test, but Dad's in a good mood. Now's my chance.

As we're walking out of the mall, I casually say, "So Dad, I was thinking, since Gene has his dialysis appointment on Friday, would it be all right if he and I went camping? He only has to go to his appointments once every three days, so he'd be good all weekend."

I heard somewhere that liars don't look you in the eyes and they fidget and scratch their neck. When Dad turns to me, I'm staring right at him with my hands in my pockets.

"Camping?"

"Yeah, it's near Pocatello." I hand him a printout from my pocket. "Check it out. Gene really wanted to explore the Minnetonka Cave. And there are all types of animals to see, like moose, mule deer, bison, mountain lion, and pronghorn."

Thank you, Wikipedia.

"Camping." He says it this time like he's considering it.

I force down a smile and say, "And if anything does happen to Gene, there are guides all over the place. It's really good for the old people. It's the —"

"Yeah, the Targhee National Forest. Gene took me there when I was a kid. Beautiful country." But then he sighs. "I can't do it."

Huh?

All defensive, I say, "But they have, like, a million benches for Gene if he gets tired. And there isn't a single grizzly bear in all of Idaho."

"Your grandfather is in bad shape."

"Not for this." God, I'm practically whining. "You promised. Don't break your promise."

"I said we'd go visit Gramps in Rock Springs. I never said anything about camping."

My jaw clenches. I know Dad just wants to make sure we're safe, but I'm fighting back this flood of feelings. Then I just start blubbering. "I do everything you ask. I get a B plus on my test, I don't do drugs or hang out with the wrong crowd. I even gave up the hunting trip and found a safe alternative. I'm not a kid anymore. I can take care of Gene if anything happens. Why can't you just let me do this one thing?"

Wow. I've never lied so hard in my life. My performance was so convincing that tears are welling in *my* eyes. And I want to feel like it's a good thing and the ends justify the means and all that fun stuff. I'm not doing anything wrong. I was promised this hunting trip, and this lie will fulfill Dad's promise.

Yes, it's a good thing. And I shouldn't feel so awful about it.

He looks at me like a proud parent sending his only son off to war and says, "Be safe. Please, for the love of God, be safe."

He believes me. He actually believes me.

I think I'm going to be sick.

CHAPTER 15

Wad

My alarm goes off, but I've been awake all night staring at the clock, waiting for six thirty to come. My heart didn't let me sleep. It was pounding all night, and no matter how much I read Gene's bear book, no matter how many push-ups and sit-ups I did in my room, I couldn't tire myself out. It's because I'm excited. Tomorrow morning we're leaving for the Grand Tetons. I'm not scared that Sandy might eat me or that Gene will get sick and die. No, I'm just excited because I've been waiting for this trip for so long. I'm not going to look into the fact that today is Halloween. It's not a bad sign. I mean, this is my favorite holiday of the year.

I take a lot of deep breaths in the shower, staring at the bottle of shampoo. Two hunters from Ohio got killed. It's crazy that a bear would do that. Why did she do that? Bears rarely attack humans. They were just hanging out in their tent and then bam, they're dead.

I turn off the shower. I towel off my hair. I can't believe I didn't know bulls were male elk. I told Karen that I'm this awesome hunter, but there isn't anything on my profile except for a couple of pictures of me at karaoke and my two-year-old profile pic of Brighton with his arm around my shoulder after ultimate Frisbee.

Oh, yeah, I should take that pic down. Or at least crop him out.

Last year me and Bright dressed up as Dumb and Dumber. We went to the Goodwill and I found a suit the color of orange smoothies and he picked out one that was baby blue. Everyone thought we had the best costumes, even if the suits were too big on us. Back then, Bright's hair was perfect for Harry.

We've dressed up for Halloween together for as long as I can remember. We've been Ren and Stimpy, Bloo and Mac, and we started it off in first grade with Bert and Ernie. This will be the first year that I'm going solo.

Fully decked out in my costume, I'm crossing the street when I see Bright with his friends all dressed as zombies.

"Who the heck is that?" says Timmy. His idea of a

costume is a Led Zeppelin hoodie, old sneakers, and some cheap zombie makeup from a kit.

"Tyson?" Bright says, one eyebrow raised. The zit on his nose isn't covered up today.

"Dude," Nico says, impressed. "Is this like, skinned from an actual bear?" He touches one of the canines hanging over my brow.

"Could be," I say.

Nico laughs, but Bright just stands there looking dead. He says to his friends, "I'll meet up with you guys."

After his friends walk away, Bright gives me this shameful face and says, "You got to stop this."

"Stop what?"

"You know. All this bear stuff."

"Whatever. My costume is sweet."

"You look ridiculous."

"What about that massive zit on your nose?"

He scowls.

"Uh-oh. Look out. Angry bear!" I know he hates it when I say "bear" after everything. He shoves me, but I hold my ground. He's not looking at me. He's looking over my shoulder.

I turn around and his friends are watching us from three houses down. How can I humiliate him like he did to me?

I lock him in a bear hug and we fall into the grass.

"Get off me!" He's swinging punches, but my costume cushions the blows. And I'm laughing because he can't get up.

I say, "Not until you admit you like Taylor Swift." I hack up a wad of snot and hold it in. The shadow of my costume's teeth are on his face.

His eyes widen. "Don't."

The wad dangles out my smile.

He says, "Dude, seriously. Cut it out." He squirms and fights, but that only makes the wad wiggle.

I can't stop laughing and the thread is getting thinner. And longer.

With his face turned and eyes closed, he says, "I like some of her stuff."

"Louder," I carefully say.

He shouts, "'Mean' is my favorite song!"

"Who wrote it?"

"Taylor Swift!"

But it's too late. The thread breaks . . . all over his face.

"Gah!"

I release him and he wipes the wad away, smearing it onto the grass.

"You're a liar," I say. "And you're pathetic."

He smiles because he knows I'm talking about his all-time favorite song. And mine. He says, "Why do you have to be so mean?"

"Remember that time you wiped your booger on me in first grade? Now we're even."

He scrunches his face until it dawns on him. "Oh, yeah. You came over after school. Remember when my mom wouldn't let us play soccer until we picked up Chloe's poo?"

"So we grabbed some shovels and chucked it into your neighbor's yard."

For the first time in forever, he does his British guffaw.

I look over. Bright's friends have left.

He says, "Have you been working out?" And now he's just being sarcastic.

I shake my head and walk away, because he just won't stop sucking. I'm not going to deal with it anymore.

"Timmy says you drew me a picture," he says from about ten steps behind.

"Just leave me alone."

"A bear kicking a football." He laughs.

I walk faster. "It was an assignment. We had to draw a friend or a family member as an animal. Ms. Davis is weird."

"Do you remember in elementary school when you were Pizza Bear? What was I? Booger Bear?"

"Booger Bear Five Thousand."

"Oh, yeah. We were so ridiculous."

I cross the last intersection before school, and the first bus is pulling up to the front door. Bright is still walking behind me and it's so awkward. Finally he says, "Have you, uh, noticed we don't really hang out anymore?"

"Nah, missed it." I open the door. I don't hold it for him.

"Because I was thinking you could come over and we could play air hockey."

He really can't think I'd fall for that again.

He grabs me by the shoulder. "Hey, man, I only told them about you because Timmy kept bugging me. You know, he was giving me a hard time because we lost the last two games by a field goal. And he had this big ski trip to Steamboat with his parents, and he wasn't going to invite me unless I went along with his stupid plan." And then he says, "It killed me, dude."

Part of me doesn't trust him, but most of me really thinks he's just as big of a dork as I am.

He says, "How can I make it up to you?"

"I don't know. I just . . . I mean, would you be able to forgive me if I did that to you?"

He looks sorry, kinda like Chloe did when he scolded

her for getting into his Chipotle. And then finally he goes, "Hey, um, when you get back from Wyoming, I'll do whatever you say. I bear swear."

"Huh?" I wasn't expecting those two words to come out of his mouth.

He smiles. "Karen showed it to Mika. Mika showed me. Everyone's doing it now."

I shrug. "I am a trendsetter."

"Oh, yeah? Is 'yamhole' catching on?"

"I've heard a few people say it."

"*No one* is saying it."

"Yeah, I know."

He's laughing a bunch and I really want to laugh too, but I can't make it seem like we're suddenly cool again.

"So can we still be friends?" And then he sweetens the deal with "It would be totally yam."

He's right about that, but who's to say that he won't betray me again?

The bell rings.

"I don't know," I say.

Outside the auditorium, he tries to do the bear swear with me, but I'm not having any of it. So he clumsily bumps his fists with my paws. And then he turns and stumbles away like a wiener. He looks like he did in first grade when he didn't know how to talk American and everyone made fun of him and he only had one friend.

God, I better not get all soft on him.

I step into the auditorium, and Mr. Cavner says, "Have a seat, Tyson." He's searching through the desk drawers on stage and wearing a red Mr. Rogers sweater-vest. But it's not a costume. He always kinda looks like Mr. Rogers. "We'll pick up where we left off yesterday."

Karen's jaw drops when she sees me, but she still holds her smile. She's dressed up as a hunter — camouflage jacket and pants, and an orange vest. I want to sit next to her, but the only seat left is on the other side of the auditorium near the door. During the entire period, she's sneaking glances at me, quickly turning away whenever I catch her.

After class lets out, I slowly put my things away, timing it just right so she'll pass me as I'm standing up.

"Hi, Bear," she says, and we walk out of the auditorium together.

"Hi, Hunter. I like your costume."

"Thanks. I actually wore this at Five-J. I didn't really need to, though. I shot that oryx from a pickup."

"They don't keep any of my kind at those ranches, do they?"

"You mean grizzlies? No, I haven't hunted any bears . . . yet." She winks.

Oh, my God, that's got to be a signal. "Yup, I'm going to be riding horseback where those two hunters from Ohio got killed."

"And you're not freaked out?"

"Nah. All you have to do is make a lot of noise and you scare them right off."

She shakes her head. "You'd never see me in a place like that. Gives me the creeps just thinking about it. Grizzly bears aren't anything to be messing around with, not in my book."

"So, I was wondering, do you want to do something next week?"

With a sly look she goes, "You asking me out?"

"No. Well, yes. Kind of. You ever done karaoke?"

"No, never been."

"It's so much fun."

"Just don't get eaten this weekend."

"Are you trying to scare me?"

"I'm just saying that if that bear attacks, do *not* run,

because they charge at thirty miles an hour. If you run, you have no chance. No, you gotta play dead. Lie on the ground with your head down and keep your hands behind your neck. Better odds of survival."

I fake a laugh, but all those words of warning I read in Gene's book sound so much more . . . real . . . coming out of her mouth. "Stop messing with me." My voice has suddenly become frail.

"Grizzly bears are the strongest land animals on earth. I want to go on a date with *one* you. Not a hundred pieces of you." She hugs me in the middle of hallway traffic, and I've never felt anything more comforting and terrifying at the same time.

Karen's seriously concerned face is inches from mine, and it hits me like a neck-snapping blow to the face: I got a date with the girl of my dreams, but I'll probably be dead before the weekend is up.

CHAPTER 16

It's Hot and Uncomfortable
Inside a Bear

I check the news on my phone in American Civ, and they haven't found Sandy. Usually when a bear harms someone, the Forest Service puts it down, because once they attack one human, they become more likely to attack another. But she just vanished.

Horrible thoughts are running through my mind as I walk home. Maybe wearing this bear costume is symbolic in some way. Like the universe is sending me a message. I'm inside a bear now, just like I will be after I get eaten by one in Wyoming.

I am thinking way too deep. This is so unlike me. I am thinking about death and what it feels like to have teeth wrapped around my neck when I should be picturing a fun-filled trip with Gene — riding horses, bonding over our kills, and filling our heads with memories we will never forget.

This could be my last day alive.

I have to get out of this ridiculous bear suit.

When I get home, Dad is hauling his suitcase down the stairs.

"Hey, you're looking pretty ferocious there, Tyson. You ready to go to Rock Springs?"

I nod.

"What's wrong? You don't seem excited."

"Oh, no. It's just, I got a lot of things on my mind."

"What's going on?"

"It's nothing important."

"You sure?"

"No, really, Dad. I'm fine."

"You know you can talk to me if something's bothering you."

"I know. Nothing's bothering me."

He doesn't look convinced. "Well, let's get going."

"Just let me change."

"I thought you were going to wear that bear costume all day."

"It's hot and uncomfortable."

"But you're going to wear it tonight with your grandfather, right?"

"I don't know."

"You don't *know*? You spent all that money."

"Dad, please. Let me go change."

I'm making for the staircase when he says, "Did you
pack all of Gramps's camping equipment?"

"Yes, Dad."

"His tent? His cooler?"

"Yes."

"And warm clothes? It's going to be cold in Idaho."

"I packed everything."

"Come here." He pulls me into a half hug, one hand
around my shoulder. "I'm sorry."

"For what?"

"For treating you like a child. You're more mature than
I gave you credit for. I was really apprehensive about the
hunt because even though you're not Gene's grandson,
you are my son. If you're anything like me, you would have
fainted when you saw all the blood and guts. There is a lot
of it in an animal that size."

"You fainted?"

"Your gramps—Gene—poured his canteen on me to wake me up."

I'm not like Dad. I'm not scared about cutting open an animal as big as a morbidly obese dude or getting blood on my hands. I won't faint out there.

I really hope I don't faint.

I laugh. "Wuss."

"And you understand why you're not going on the hunt, right?"

"Because Gene is sick."

"I don't know what I would do if something happened to either of you. I love you guys so much." He wraps his arm around my neck and pulls me in for a painful noogie, giving a growl.

"Dad. Cut it out."

I have this heavy lump of guilt sitting low in my stomach. I mean, he doesn't want me to go to the Grand Tetons for all the right reasons. But I'm going for all the right reasons, too.

Mom, Dad, and Ashley are planning on doing the whole tourist thing near Rock Springs—visit the wild horse sanctuary in the Red Desert, then the Killpecker Sand Dunes. Dad's even talking about renting some ATVs to go off-roading, but I'll believe it when I see it. If Gene and I make it back on Sunday, they'll take me home.

When we get to the nursing home, Mom and Dad help bring our gear into the lobby.

Dad goes, "Call our cell if anything happens, you hear?"

"We will." Gene told me there isn't an ounce of signal in the Tetons.

"If Gene starts to feel weak or ill, if he gets a headache or is short of breath, I want you two to go to a ranger station immediately. Be responsible."

Mom rolls her eyes. "Oh, Lee, they'll be fine."

Dad smiles, nodding in agreement. "Most important, I want you two to have a good time."

Dad gives me a hug and Mom kisses my forehead, then they get in the SUV and drive away.

Gene is finishing dinner by himself in the cafeteria. He's wearing his cowboy hat. He wears it every year when he drives to the Tetons. It has a raven's feather, cigarette burns, and bloodstains.

He wipes his mouth with a napkin, and his sleeve slides up his arm. There's a bandage barely covering a large bruise on his right forearm.

"What happened?" I say.

"Dialysis appointment this morning."

"Oh."

Knowing Gene, he was probably just sitting in a reclining chair and chatting with his nurse about the weather, like it's no big deal that blood is getting pumped in and out of his body.

The thought of all that blood and the white hospital room and the beeping machine noises makes my head go light. Black spots appear around my vision. I have to sit down. I'm such a wuss.

And I'm definitely Dad's son.

In fourth grade, my entire class surrounded a table to watch Mr. Carmichael dissect a cow eyeball and talk about all the different parts. When the knife went in and the juices squirted, everything went black. The next thing I remembered, I was on the ground and everyone was looking down at me. Mr. Carmichael put a cold rag on my forehead.

I had fainted. It was so embarrassing.

Maybe Dad was right. Gene is going to be mauled by Sandy, and he'll be screaming for me to help him, but I'll be passed out and useless in the sagebrush.

"Gene, am I a man?"

"Nope," he says, without giving it a second thought.

"I thought you said thirteen is the year boys become men."

He shrugs. "I know boys who are five times your age."

"So hunting makes you into one?"

He shakes his head. "I know just the thing to cheer you up." He takes off his cowboy hat and places it on my head. He says, "You can be me for Halloween."

CHAPTER 17

The Grand Tetons

Gene goes to bed right after *Jeopardy!* and I stay up doing sit-ups and push-ups in the cramped living room. When my muscles can't even lift me off the ground, I crawl onto the really small couch and put on his *Two and a Half Men* Season 3 DVD, but there's no way I'll fall asleep with Gene snoring in the other room like he's got a Tater Tot stuck in his throat.

It's after midnight and I've gone through all the episodes on disc 1, and it returns to the main screen. I can't find the remote and I'm so scared that I can't even get up to turn off the TV, so they're playing the theme song on repeat.

"Men men men men, manly men men men."

For three hours.

"*Men men men men, manly men men men, oo hoo hoo, hoo hoo, oo.*"

A real man wouldn't be curled up like a fetus, hoping that morning never comes. I'm not even half a man.

We leave the nursing home at four a.m., and I maybe got fifteen minutes of sleep. The sun rises just as we pass through Jackson, the last city before the national forest. There isn't a single car on the road. On our left-hand side, the Teton mountains rise up epically from the surrounding prairie, and they're orange from the rising sun. Any other time, I would be amazed by these sights, but with death hovering overhead like a starving vulture, everything feels drab and colorless.

We get stopped by a herd of buffalo crossing the road. They look like devil creatures with their hooked horns and giant flat faces. A huge bull shepherding three calves stares at us menacingly.

I roll down my window to take a picture of them with my phone, but then I catch my reflection in the rearview mirror. With Gene's lucky hat, I kinda look like a real cowboy. I make a serious face and sneak a picture of myself instead.

When the buffalo pass, Gene takes a right and we enter into a forest of pine and aspen. The sign reads: GROS VENTRE ROAD.

"How do you say that?"

"*Grow-vaunt.* It's French for 'Big Belly.' Yup, just twenty or so miles down this road and we'll be at the ranch."

The narrow road winds and climbs up out of the forest, and now we're on a mountainside with a steep cliff to our right. There is no barricade, nothing to prevent us from falling hundreds of feet into the massive lake at the bottom.

Gene pulls over to the shoulder as an oncoming truck appears from beyond a bend.

"I'm gonna take a leak," he says, then gets out.

I open the door to join him, but a small piece of ground comes loose beneath my foot and tumbles down the cliff. I guess I can hold it until we get to the ranch.

Gene looks like he's in pain as he gets back in.

"You okay?" I say.

"I'm fine." He breathes in deep a few times and blinks a bunch, like he just spaced out. He gets back on the road, which is getting worse the farther along we go. As we go higher up, the ride gets so bumpy I can feel the vibrations.

He coughs and his eyes get red.

"You sure you're okay?"

"Of course."

The vibrations get so extreme that the truck slides at a curve, then tips a little on my side. Gene presses harder on the gas, and the engine revs up. I grab onto the handle above the window, squeeze my eyes shut, and brace for whatever's going to happen next.

Gene gives a nervous laugh. "That'll wake you up."

I open my eyes. My hands are tingling and cold. Everything's okay.

Snow begins to fall.

What if no one's at the ranch? What if there aren't any horses? Or worse, what if there isn't even a *ranch*? We're going to be stuck out in the middle of nowhere with a broken-down truck and no one to rescue us.

And then Sandy will come.

When the road levels out, I say, "Ashley was afraid that we might run into a grizzly bear."

"Are you afraid of grizzlies?" he asks.

"No. Of course not."

"They scare me to death. Haven't I told you my grizz encounter stories?"

"You told me one decapitated your horses."

There's this deepness to his eyes like he's looking at his memories instead of the road. He always gets excited at a chance to tell a story. "There was this other time I was hunting with some coworkers and we rode up to this place called Hackamore."

Hackamore Creek. That's where the Oklahoma girl got her legs broken.

He continues, "We got off our horses, and my guide and I went up a hillside that was covered in this really thick black timber. We were climbing over felled trees, hacking through overgrowth and branches. When we reached the top of this hill, we found the elk herd. There must have been close to two dozen. Just as I'm aiming my rifle, they all take off running. Then this big, mean bear — and she was solid. Just pure muscle. She comes huffing out of the trees —"

"How big was she?"

"*Big.* Like a couple of idiots, we haul it down that hillside, and sure enough we see her following us. We're screaming and hollering for our lives, and she finally backed off when she saw the other hunters at the bottom of the hill."

"Was it Sandy?"

"Yup. She was mean even back then."

"I thought bears normally leave people alone."

"This one don't like people."

"Why?"

He nibbles at one of his fingernails, then rolls down the window and spits it out. Maybe because he's nervous, too. "Some bears are just nasty."

"Do you think we'll see her?"

"I usually see her once every other year. Flip a coin. Heads we see her and tails we don't." He hands me a penny from his cup holder.

I flick the coin, catch it, and smack it against the top of my hand.

"So what is it?" he asks.

It's Abraham Lincoln's decapitated head.

CHAPTER 18

Grizzly Bears Like Their Meat Rotten

Our ranch is the very last on the road. With its tractors and flatbed trailers rusting away in overgrown grass, this place would be perfect for a horror movie.

Gene stops at the locked metal gate, and an engine growls to life next to the barn about a football field's length away. An ATV hurries through the pasture where horses are grazing in the snow and stops on the other side of the gate.

"Hello, there," the guy says. He's stout and tall, maybe midfifties, and wearing a camouflage hat backward. "The name's Mike."

"Pleasure to meet you. I'm Gene and this is Tyson."

"Marjorie told me all about you two. Said you're looking to fill your tags. Well, Sunday is the last day of the season, so you better get to it."

"How have the elk been?" Gene asks.

"Saw a pretty decent herd going up Hackamore yesterday."

Would everyone please stop saying that name?

Mike gets the combination for the lock and swings the gate open. "Make yourself at home. Me and my girl just got breakfast made. You guys like elk sausage?"

"Tyson loves it," Gene replies. And on any other day, he would be right. But for the first time in forever, I've completely lost my appetite. Just the idea of food is enough to make my stomach clench.

"Nancy will saddle you up some horses." He points out into the pasture. "That painted horse over there, that's Ellie. Real big, but she's a sweetheart. You can ride her, Gene. And Tyson, I got a good one picked out for you."

"Is mine going to be a sweetheart, too?"

With an unsettling grin he says, "I'll put you on Crazy Eyes."

Oh, man, that time I rode on horseback during our fifth-grade camping trip, I had no idea what I was doing. The other kids were laughing as my horse wandered away from the rest of the group. Our guide was yelling at me to steer her back, and then I did something wrong, because she started galloping and I fell off.

There's no way I'll be able to control a crazy horse.

Mike shows us to the cookshack, which is a big log cabin with a fully working kitchen powered by a generator and a water pump. It also has two small beds right next to the dining table. I just want to stay in here, make a fire, sit back with a full stomach, and maybe read some more of my bear book. But there's no time — Mike's girlfriend, Nancy, is already saddling our horses.

After Gene finishes his breakfast and I force down a sausage link and half a glass of OJ, I hear the clomping of horses. Through the window, there's a large brown horse and a horse with black and white spots like a dairy cow.

Me and Gene put on our orange safety vests and head outside.

Nancy, a pretty woman maybe ten years younger than Mike, gets off my horse. And now I understand why my horse is called Crazy Eyes. Her eyes are shockingly blue and wide, with the whites showing, like she's spooked and about to do something unpredictable.

"Gene, you want to trade?" I say.

"Huh?"

"I was just thinking, you know, that you got a little more experience with horses."

"Let your grandfather ride Ellie," Nancy says. "You don't want him falling off and breaking a hip, do you?"

"No."

She smiles. "Why don't you hop on? Let's see if she likes you."

So with one foot in a stirrup, I grab the horn and hoist myself over the saddle. Crazy Eyes doesn't make any sudden movements. She's just hanging out.

"Hey there, cowboy," Gene says. "You look like a natural."

Yeah. People ride horses all the time. I can do this.

"What did you expect?" I say, and even if they can see right through me, no one says a thing.

Nancy ties the lead rope to the horn and hands me the leather reins. "You know the commands?"

"Uh . . ."

"Pull back to slow down — but don't pull back too hard. Give her a kick in the belly when you want her to go. Take these reins, and left goes left and right goes right."

"Got your rifles in the scabbards," Mike says. "You've shot a gun before, Tyson?"

"Oh, yeah. We used to go to the shooting range all the time."

"Well, all right, then. Gene, you know the country pretty well?"

After three tries, Gene mounts his horse. He looks weak and dizzy, blinking a bunch as he grabs the reins. He says, "Yes, sir. I've been hunting out of the ranch at Cottonwood the last sixteen seasons. When I worked with Henry Feed and Tractor, Martin and I hunted right out of here."

"Any word on that bear?" I say to Mike.

"Sandy?" He shakes his head. "Haven't found her yet. TV stations were all over here a couple'a days ago."

Nancy says, "You two keep your eyes peeled, won't you?"

"We'll be fine," Gene says.

"She's an old bear," Mike says. "Nasty, too. But it'll be a sad day when the Forest Service finally tracks her down. She's just as much of the park as anything else."

I say, "So she's just that way for no apparent reason?"

Nancy and Mike look at each other, thinking about the question. Finally Mike goes, "There was an incident where one of her cubs got shot."

"Really?"

"We'll chitchat later," Gene says, annoyed, and he starts down the trail toward the wooden fence. A large orange sign reads: *You are now entering the national park. No motorized vehicles. Trail open to horse and foot travel only.*

I squeeze Crazy Eyes's belly with my foot, and she gets her head right behind Ellie's butt.

Don't be nervous. Horses can sense fear, and they act on it.

I say to Gene, "You sure you're feeling okay?"

"I'm top-notch. You're not chickening out, are you?"

"No, no. I mean, what are we going to do if something goes wrong and we're like three miles from the ranch?"

"I've been hunting every season since I was your age, and I know this country better than you know your video games. Let's have Tyson worry about Tyson and Gene worry about Gene. Sound good?"

An uncomfortable silence fills the gap between us as we take a trail through the snow-dusted sagebrush. There's a hill to our left and a drop-off to our right. The path tightens, and at this point, I don't have to worry about my horse wanting to go nuts and take off, because there's no room. There are, however, quite a few more things for me to worry about. What if my horse loses her footing? What if—?

Okay. I need to calm down. If something does happen, I can't be freaking out.

Gene veers to the right and goes down the drop-off, his horse taking slower, more cautious steps toward a creek that babbles and winds past a hill.

My horse follows.

I grab the horn tight and I'm leaning my body backward, trying to balance myself with my horse. "Where are we going?"

Gene points between two very big hills in the distance. "You see that valley?"

"Is that Hackamore?"

"Hackamore is three valleys past that."

How am I going to ride for that long? My legs are already aching and my back hurts. "Oh."

The horses clomp and splash on the river rocks. And then Crazy Eyes hoists herself onto dry land. Her body brushes up against the willow bushes. Branches are snapping, and this most definitely is not a path.

Gene goes, "In these parts, you learn your way around by the creeks. This one is called Fish Creek. The one up in that valley ahead, that's North Fork. Then you got Purdy. And after that it'll be another half mile to Hackamore. If you get lost, follow the flow of the water and it'll lead you back to the ranch."

"Gene?"

"Yes, sir?"

"Hackamore is dark timber, right?"

"Oh, would you quit worrying about bears? Your horse will know if one's around."

"What will she do?"

"You'd better hold on to her neck tight, because she's gonna haul ass."

"I want to go home," I mutter. My words vanish into the sounds of the creek, the clomp of the horses' hooves, and the screeching of a hawk over our heads.

We move forward.

"Yeah, it's getting to be about that time of year. Grizzes are trying to get real nice and fat before they go into hibernation." He points up at the hawk. "And when you see birds like that, you can bet the house there's a dead animal somewhere around."

I remember what he told me: *Grizzly bears like their meat rotten.*

Gene lifts his head up, sniffing the air. "You smell that?"

"What?"

"The musk."

"I don't smell anything."

"That's elk. They must have gone through here." He points to tracks in a patch of snow to his left and all excited, he says, "You see that? Elk tracks."

"So maybe we won't have to go all the way to Hackamore?"

"They don't come out to feed in the brush until sunrise and sunset. We want to get to Hackamore by six. That will be our best bet to snag our bull."

Out here, Gene seems more himself, more alert. He knows everything about this country, and that's one of the things that's making me not have a full-fledged panic attack.

Actually, it's the only thing.

We find our way back onto a trail and head toward the valley. The trail disappears into a thicket of trees.

"We're going in there?" I say.

He turns his head and glances at me from the corner of his eye. He doesn't say a word.

I go, "If we run into Sandy, we can shoot her, right? Like, if she's coming to attack us?"

"Last I checked, killing a grizzly bear is a federal offense."

"But that's for sport. What if our lives are in danger?"

"Tell it to the courts. They're on the endangered-species list. If you kill a grizzly, you can get a year in prison and a fifty-thousand-dollar fine. You gotta leave the killing to the Forest Service."

"Well, I'm shooting anyway. I'd rather be in prison for a year than in a bear's stomach."

"They have a saying out here — if you're going to shoot a grizzly, make sure you have six bullets in your gun. Five for the bear, and one for yourself."

The dark timber swallows us whole.

CHAPTER 19

The Place Where the Ohio Couple Died

Every sound in these woods is a bear. A twig snaps beneath the horses' hooves — that's a bear. Gene coughs — another bear. That mockingbird chirping in the trees? Nope, that's a grizzly bear chirping in the trees.

We reach another clearing, a creek to our right, and just beyond that is a mountainside with burned and fallen trees and some small trees emerging from the thin layer of snow.

"What happened there?" I say.

"That's Burnt Ridge. A forest fire burned down the mountainside."

Our horses stop and cock their heads. With Crazy Eyes looking the way she does, I can't tell whether or not she's nervous.

"Did you hear that?" Gene says.

"No."

"You didn't hear that roar? Oh, man. There's a bear just on the other side of the ridge." He kicks his horse. "Come on. Let's keep moving."

Is he toying with me? No, Gene wouldn't do that. Besides, the horses heard it, too. My ears must not be tuned right. But if there really is a bear, how can Gene be so calm? I mean, there are a million places where one could hide.

Somewhere in this sagebrush, a couple from Ohio was asleep when Sandy tore down their tent. We could be riding over the very place where they died.

I look for bear tracks.

We cross another creek. The horses seem to know the shallowest path, but they're still up to their bellies and splashing water onto my boots.

"This is Purdy, right, Gene?"

"You're catching on."

"So what else is out here besides bear and elk?"

"Oh, lots of stuff. There's moose and deer and even a wolf pack that runs around in these parts. There used to be hundreds, then they got hunted to nothing. The Park Service reintroduced them in ninety-five."

"Are they dangerous?"

"Nah, they don't like humans. Consider yourself fortunate if you ever run into a wolf. They're very hard to come by. One thing you need to be afraid of more than the bears are moose."

"Really?"

"They'll pummel you into the ground until there's nothing left." And then he responds to my silence with "They don't call this the wilderness for nothing."

Something meaty, funky, and awful is in the air.

"You smell that?" I say.

Gene turns to me and puts his index finger to his mouth.

Oh, man. He smells it, too.

My pulse thuds in my ears. Can a thirteen-year-old have a heart attack?

Gene gets off his horse and throws a pack over his shoulder. He points to the top of the bare hill to our left.

"What is it?" I whisper.

He comes over to me. "Grab your rifle. We're going on foot from here."

"But what's that smell?"

"Elk musk. There must be a whole herd."

Gene doesn't want to spook the elk if they're on the other side of the hill, so we tie our horses to the nearest trees and go on foot. I hope they'll still have their heads when we return.

I'm exhausted just looking at the hill — it must be a quarter mile to the top. I sling my rifle over my shoulder and follow Gene's lead.

He goes, "At least we didn't have to go all the way out to Hackamore, huh?"

The more we climb, the bigger the hill gets. The air is thin, and it doesn't take long until I'm heaving and panting through my teeth. My thighs are burning, like I'm in gym class doing wall-sits. My chest aches, my calves are trembling, my stomach muscles burn, and for some random reason, even my shoulders hurt.

I take another look up to see how far we've come. We're not even halfway to the top.

I can't wuss out now. Gene just got all the blood pumped out of his body yesterday. What excuse do I have?

Out here, I *have* to be like Gene, because cereal-eating and video-game-playing Tyson won't cut it.

I know it's a bad idea, but I have to look again.

We made it?

I want to shout for joy, but I fall into the sagebrush, my chest heaving against the ground.

"Tyson," Gene says.

Every word is a struggle to get out. "Shouldn't you be whispering?"

"The elk aren't here. We'll stick around and wait for sunset. They'll be back." He holds out a hand and helps me sit up. "Hopefully."

Whoa. From up here, it's like I can see all the never-ending Wyoming wilderness. Purdy is as thin as a strand of angel-hair pasta, and the bare hilltops and the tree-filled valleys look pale, like when the color filter on my TV is turned down. And the sky is so much bigger than the sky back home. But why is that? It's the same sky.

This is the elks' home. And the bears' home. This is why we lied to my parents and why we pruned and why Gene was willing to shell out thousands of dollars.

It's not like I haven't traveled before. I've seen the Pacific Ocean and the fantasy-world trees of Sequoia National Forest. But the whole time, either Dad would be taking pictures or Mom would be making sure me and Ashley were wearing enough layers, and it was all so . . . safe. I always knew the SUV and my PlayStation PSP were waiting in the parking lot.

But today, it's just me, an old man, and Mother Nature.

"This is unreal," I say, catching my breath. "We climbed this high?"

Gene unzips his pack and hands me a sandwich wrapped in plastic, a small bag of chips, and a Coke. He says, "Pretty cool, ain't it?"

"Man, this is amazing."

He takes a bite of his sandwich and says, "I'm really glad you came out here. Hunting is a dying sport. All you kids nowadays are used to your food packaged up at the grocery store and your nature on television."

I nod. I'm just trying to take this all in.

He says, "Meatballs don't grow on trees. An animal has to die." With pride in his eyes, he says, "I'm so glad you're going to experience that. To the Shoshone Indians, the elk symbolized stamina, freedom, and nobility. It is a great honor to kill an elk, and I want you to appreciate that."

"I do, Gene. But . . . meatball trees?"

"Don't you remember when you were nine and you planted your grandmother's meatballs? You were trying to grow a meatball tree."

"Oh, yeah. It didn't grow. That was right after she died, wasn't it?"

"She made spaghetti the night before she had the stroke, and she put the leftovers in the freezer. You loved her meatballs so much and you knew no one would ever make them like she did."

"I remember you helped me water it."

He laughs. "Your father must have thought we were nuts."

"You really loved her."

He's smiling, and this isn't the same person I saw by himself and all skinny in the nursing home. This is the guy I grew up with, the guy who would finish Grandma's crossword puzzles and get annoyed at her for taking forever to open her Christmas presents. His eyes get deep and young-looking and he says, "You know she hunted with me for twenty-some-odd years?"

"No way. Grandma was a *hunter*?"

"She had a shot like you wouldn't believe."

Maybe it is in my blood, then.

He says, "She came up with the bear swear. I promised her we'd come out here every year, and I always kept my word."

After I've finished my lunch, I lay Gene's cowboy hat on the snow and pick at a sagebrush plant between my feet.

"Hey, Gene? So what's the deal with my real grandfather? Dad didn't want to talk about him."

"That's because Lawrence was a bad person. He did not treat your family well."

"Lawrence? That's his name?"

"Your grandma was the secretary for Henry Feed and Tractor. When she came into work with bruises on her face, I called the police. Lawrence had a trailer on his property where he was cooking meth. The judge sent him to prison for twenty years."

"My grandfather was a meth head?"

Gene nods.

"Ha. Wow. That explains a lot."

"When I met your father, he was eight years old, and boy, was he a timid kid. It took some time for him to warm up to me. I found out Lawrence had abused him."

"He *what*?"

"One time he got sent to the hospital for a broken arm because Lawrence pushed him down the staircase."

This is a joke. I mean, it has to be a joke and I want to laugh, but my chest sinks low and I feel dirty and strange knowing this about Dad. But Gene isn't joking. I will never look at Dad the same way again.

I say, "Is that why you guys didn't tell me about . . . you know. You."

He sighs. "You're a lot like your father — thoughtful, caring —"

"You mean weak."

"I mean you both have big hearts. Christ, the *biggest*

of hearts. Saying you're like your dad isn't a bad thing. I meant it as a compliment. Family means a lot to you. I don't know many children who'd consider a guy like me as a friend. That is, except for your dad. When he was your age, he called me his best friend, too. He didn't want to ruin that for you."

As dorky and as lame as he is, I actually have a really good dad. He loves Gene; he loves Mom and Ashley and me. Not everyone can say that. Some people have horrible dads.

I say, "I, uh . . . I was talking to Dad the other day and I mentioned home dialysis."

"That's expensive, Tyson."

"I know. But, you know, what if we sold the house and all moved into a small apartment together?"

He smiles. "You'd have to share a room with Ashley. Are you willing to make that kind of sacrifice?"

"Well, yeah. I mean, how many people in a nursing home can still ride horseback and hunt elk? You don't belong there. Please, let's sell the house and get you the machine."

He shakes his head. "I owe more on the house than it's worth. Believe me, your father and I looked at all my options. Sunrise Village is what we can afford."

I don't really know what to say. Or think. I'm not sad or

upset anymore. I just feel . . . old. Like one day all of this is going to happen to me.

The sun falls below a hill, and a really cold wind hits me. I look down at our horses, and from up here they're the size of those plastic cowboy and Indian toys Grandma used to get me. But in the clearing on the opposite side, something big is lurking in the sagebrush.

Gene whispers, "Crouch down. Get your rifle ready."

I'm squinting, but I can't make out what kind of beast that is. "What is it?"

"A six-point."

CHAPTER 20

Where Everything I Wanted Comes True

I'm lying on the ground. The butt of my rifle is pressed firmly against my shoulder, and I switch off the safety. Through my magnifying scope, I see more elk step out of the woods. First dozens and then hundreds. I've never seen so many animals together like this. These giant deer look mythical; they make me feel like I've stepped into a fantasy world. They look nothing like the computer-generated images in Great American Hunter 5.

This is incredible.

"Get a six-point," Gene whispers, lying on the ground ten feet from me. "Shoot him right in the shoulder."

But I can't. These elk are way cooler than I could ever be.

This is what Gene waits for every year. We came out here to kill a beautiful animal.

"No. You go first," I say.

"Don't chicken out now."

"I'm *not.*"

"Come on, they're two hundred yards away."

I search through the herd and find a huge bull in the middle of a bunch of elk cows. I count his points. Six. He's what we came here for.

I adjust myself, steadying my rifle in the dirt. The bull is in the center of my crosshairs.

Gene says, "What are you waiting for?"

If I want to be a real hunter, I shouldn't be hiding in the shrub two hundred yards away with a rifle. No, we should be duking it out in hand-to-hoof combat to see who truly is the stronger animal.

"Tyson!"

My finger tightens and I fire, the butt of my rifle hitting my shoulder.

The six-point jerks his head up and takes off into the clearing, a blur among the rest of the stampede.

"I got him!" A shot of adrenaline and regret empties into my blood. My hands are tingling and my ears are ringing, and whether or not I should have killed the elk doesn't matter. 'Cause I did it.

"Shoot him again!"

"What? Why?"

"You hit him in the gut."

"So?"

Gene fires into the air and my bull changes course.

He says, "Right there. He's by himself."

Aiming at a moving target is really hard. I give him a lead and fire again, but I'm way off. He vanishes into a dense clump of forest. The valley echoes with gunfire, the air gets thick with gunpowder, and all the elk have cleared out.

"Christ," Gene says.

"What's the matter? I got him."

"He's still alive. We have to go find him."

"What about your elk?"

Gene throws his rifle down. "Dammit, Tyson! How many times have I told you — you got to shoot them in the shoulder?"

But I tried. My hands were shaking, and I had never shot an elk before. None of that matters. "I — I'm sorry. We can still get him. Right?"

He looks at the sky, and it's getting dark fast. "Let's go. We've only got about forty-five minutes."

"If it's too dangerous, let's just go back. I mean, it's not the end of the world if we don't bring home an elk."

His lips purse into an angry scowl. "You want to let

that animal suffer? He could still be alive for hours, slowly bleeding out his stomach. It's your responsibility that he dies humanely."

He's right—we can't leave the bull like this. An animal is in agony because of me. I take the headlamp out of Gene's pack and put it around my forehead. I sling my rifle over my shoulder and march down the hill.

Gene brings his handgun. It has six chambers for six bullets.

I wanted this. I wanted these freezing hands and this guilt and terror and a million other awful feelings jabbing my chest. I wanted to hang out with this old man and prove myself. But what does that even mean? What do I have to prove? Did I shoot that elk because Bright isn't my friend anymore, or because I had to show Mom and Dad that I'm not a kid? I mean . . . am I really that childish?

I don't deserve to be wearing Gene's cowboy hat.

A trail of blood leads into the trees, and it's almost entirely night in there, even though there's still some sunlight where I'm standing. Gene steps in front of me, but I won't let him go first. It's my fault we're hiking into this mess of trees.

I listen for a moving animal, but the only sounds are the dead leaves and snow beneath our feet. Where do we go? It's too dark and there's too much stuff everywhere to see a blood trail. Ahead of us is a mostly clear path. To my right, the woods go up a hill and all the branches are tangled in an impenetrable web.

When elk get wounded, they go into the densest woods possible to hide from predators. So I take a right, fighting my way through branches that scratch my face and arms. I climb up, then slip down a rock. My knee screams in pain. I don't make a sound.

Gene doesn't say anything. He just follows my lead. His breathing is very loud, but he doesn't complain.

How far did the elk go? Gene said he once had to follow a dying elk for three miles. But that was during the morning, and they had all afternoon to find him.

A spatter of blood is black in the snow next to a tree stump. We're going the right way, but I don't feel any relief knowing that.

I don't know how long we climb up the hillside. Maybe five minutes? There's still a little bit of light blue in the west, but not enough to get us out of here even if we left right now.

I turn on my headlamp, and an eye glistens at me. Oh, my God, it's a bear. I stumble back, falling into Gene, and we both end up against a tree.

"Tyson, for Christ's sake!" he says.

"Shhhh," I whisper. "There's a bear over there."

He yanks the headlamp from me and shines it at the eye. It's my elk. He's lying on the ground, mouth wide open, chest heaving like he's having an asthma attack. His entire belly is stained black with blood. He's looking with glassy eyes at me.

The elk squeals, and I'm so sorry. Here I am, just some kid who dresses up as a bear and jabs girls in the neck with pencil erasers, and I'm higher on the food chain than this beast?

"Where do I shoot him?" I say.

Gene gives me his handgun. "In the shoulder."

I take five paces back and aim the gun, holding it with both hands. Why is this shot so much harder than the first? The gun feels as though it weighs fifty pounds, and my hands are trembling, the muscles in my shoulders searing. I'm going to miss, or hit him in the balls, and I'm just going to make this even worse.

I fire. The bullet pings against a boulder, and the elk is still there, still dying.

"Give it to me." Gene snatches the gun, aims it with arms as unmoving as stone, and shoots. The elk twitches his leg, and then it's over.

I breathe, once, but it's not over. We're in the dark timber and there's blood everywhere and our horses are so far away.

Let the bears or the hawks take my kill. I don't want it anymore. I just want to get out of here alive.

Gene lifts up his head, looking at me, but I can't look back. "You got yourself a nice six-point here. Must be about seven hundred pounds." He reaches into his coat pocket for his digital camera, and he's suddenly a different person. He even makes a genuine smile. Doesn't he realize we're in very real danger? He says, "In all the years I've been coming out, this is one of the nicest elk I've seen. Quite an impressive feat for your first time."

One part of me is happy. Another part devastated. His six-point rack means he was probably nine or ten years old. He survived grueling winters and other hunters trying to bring him down. He probably had calves. Now his eyes are glassy and his tongue is sticking out the side of his mouth.

Gene kneels and aims the camera.

I grab the rack. The elk's head is heavy.

I should have been the one who killed him, a punishment for the pain I put him through. But instead, Gene did the dirty work, just like when he brought Dad out here.

My one moment to show Gene I could be a hunter was a disaster.

As I give the most tired smile of my life, Gene takes a picture, the flash lighting up everything. And then another. Karen and Bright and all the other kids at school are going to look at my profile next week and see me, in my orange vest and Gene's cowboy hat, holding up a dead animal's head — like a real hunter.

I thought I would be more excited than this.

I say, "How are we going to get him out of here?"

He gets a small hooked knife from the sheath around his belt. "Since this is your bull, you have the honor of field-dressing him."

"Huh?"

"We're not going to pack him out until tomorrow — it's getting too late. But if we leave his bowels in there, the meat will go rotten. So you're going to cut his belly open."

"Oh."

I breathe through my nose because I can't let Gene see just how deeply and nervously I'm breathing. Little black dots are fluttering into my eyes, and it makes these dark woods even darker. But I won't faint. I *can't* faint.

He hands me the knife.

CHAPTER 21

Like Breaking Open a Piñata

I'm going to mangle this poor animal. I can't even cut a steak without my knife slipping and getting juices on my shirt. Gene really can't expect me to just *do* this, can he? Isn't there something I can practice on first?

What if the bull's not totally dead and his legs jerk or he squeals as I cut into him?

Gene shifts the elk's massive body so the belly sticks up. With a grimace, he pulls back the left hind leg, ties a yellow rope around the hoof, and secures the other end to a tree trunk. The balls . . . and butthole are exposed. I have a knife in my hand. This isn't going to be good.

"So what you need to do is make a circular incision right around his anus."

Horror and disgust cut down my spine. "Huh?"

He smiles. He's messing with me. I make an awkward, slightly relieved laugh, and then his eyes sharpen. "Go on."

"Are you serious?"

"I don't have time to make jokes. I need you to listen now."

I nod. I ready my knife. I'm going to do whatever Gene tells me to do.

This shouldn't be a big deal. Millions of people have killed and gutted animals before me, and they never passed out because of the guts or blood. This is in my DNA. I can do this.

I stick the knife into his flesh, and I don't feel dizzy or weird yet. I just hope the elk doesn't explode all over me.

It's warm.

"Okay, good," Gene says. "Now grab the penis and make a cut toward the anus on both sides." His voice is so calm, like Ms. Davis teaching us how to make a charcoal drawing.

"Haven't we done enough to the poor guy?"

"State law. We need to prove the sex with the meat processor."

" 'Kay." And so my knife goes where he tells me, and the hide peels away.

Is this what I am? Just a pile of veins and tendons and muscle? Something that can be cut open and eaten?

What the heck am I?

Okay, breathe. Just do what Gene says.

God, this is so weird. But why does it feel so normal? And why was I afraid of this in the first place? There's blood on my hands, and I'm not dizzy at all. It smells rich and metallic and horrible, but I kinda like it.

"What do I do next?"

"Gently slit his belly up to his rib cage. Now, don't get carried away, 'cause you don't want to puncture that gut sack right there. A feather touch is all you need."

The elk rests silently on the ground. He just lies there like an obedient dog as I slide the blade up his belly. It's like his skin unzips. A large white veiny bag balloons up.

"Good. Okay, go ahead and finish your cut down to the anal cavity, making sure your knife is facing up. Careful. Don't hurt yourself."

I join my cuts together, and the gut sack comes spilling out, sliding across my foot like a really big and slimy water balloon.

This is *nothing* like breaking open a piñata.

Gene tells me every step of the way how to clean out my elk. I split open the rib cage, sever the windpipe, cut back connective tissue, and take the heart, the lungs, and the rest of his vitals out.

I'm looking at parts of the body that were never meant to see light.

The elk doesn't kick or scream. He doesn't beg for mercy. He's dead, and the only thing that moves is his fur, which fluffs gently in the breeze.

"Nice work," Gene says. "All clean cuts."

"It ain't no thang." But I feel so proud hearing him say that.

I put all the guts and organs in a pile a few feet away. A puddle of blood has collected at the bottom of the hollowed-out body. It's on my hands and arms and jeans, and I have Gene take a picture of me like this, and I make a really big smile because no one would ever believe I could do all this.

There's no way Bright could field-dress an elk. He wouldn't want to get his fancy pants all dirty.

"And last but not least . . ." Gene reaches into his pocket and pulls out a long green sticker. "It's time to tag him. Go ahead and do the honors."

I put the green sticker on his antler. He's officially mine.

It's totally dark now, and the air is so cold it hurts. The wind rustling in the willows and rattling the sagebrush reminds me that I've got blood on me and we're in the heart of Sandy's territory.

We still have to leave these woods, climb the hill, go back down to our horses, and then ride for two hours to the ranch. I'm going to sleep good tonight.

When we're heading to the horses, Gene says, "We got to get up at four a.m. and get out here at first light to pack out your elk."

People pay thousands of dollars to do this. I see why. You don't get tested like this every day.

We ride back beneath the moonlight, which casts a purple glow atop the snow cover, and it's like something out of a dream. But this is real. I've never experienced anything more vivid in my life.

I say, "Well, I guess the coin was wrong. We didn't see Sandy."

"Let's hope she doesn't get your elk before morning."

CHAPTER 22

The Smell of Elk

When we get back to the cookshack, I collapse into a deflated brown beanbag chair, my arms spread out, and when Gene calls me to eat, I don't move. I *can't*. It's past ten, and we have to be up again in six hours. But I'm going to regret it if I don't eat, so I tell my muscles and bones to quit complaining. They thank me after I get my fill of chili dogs and jalapeño potato chips.

Mike and Nancy are still awake. They tell us they can never sleep until all the hunters have returned. They sit with us in the dining area.

Nancy says, "We'll get your packhorses ready so you two can head out first thing. Gosh, a six-point. That's incredible news. Way to go, Tyson."

"Run across Sandy?" Mike says, like he knows how much the idea freaks me out.

"No bears," I say.

"That hunter who shot her cub was right around your age."

I look at Mike, and I can't tell if he's trying to test me in some way. I say, "What happened?"

He gets up from his chair and takes an old newspaper from a stack of hunting magazines next to the couch facing the fireplace. He puts it in front of me.

The headline above a yellow-highlighted article reads: "Hunter Fined Forty Thousand Dollars for Son Shooting Bear Cub."

Before I even get a chance to read, Mike says, "This kid and his dad ran into Sandy and her three cubs near Purdy Creek. The kid got scared and fired, killing one of them. Sandy never bothered anyone before that day. But ever since, she's been giving hunters problems."

"Why are you showing me this?" I say.

He looks at me dumbly. "You asked about her."

Later, I'm lying in bed, thinking. If I run into Sandy, I won't freak out and do something stupid like that kid. How could he shoot a bear cub? I mean, what the heck was running through his mind?

Maybe Sandy charged at him.

We have to haul my elk out soon. Grizzly bears can smell blood from miles away, and there's a lot of it there. First Sandy will feed, then the wolves, and whatever scraps are left over will get eaten by the hawks and eagles.

I pass out with my blood-encrusted clothes still on, so when Gene's alarm goes off, all I have to do is put on my jacket, vest, gloves, and headlamp. We snag a quick breakfast of cereal, and Gene lets me have a cup of coffee, too. But I don't need it. I'm determined to finish this job, and nothing will stop me. The smell of elk is practically tattooed on me.

I don't put Gene's hat back on because it's just going to get in the way. We march down to the barn, where our horses wait in their stalls, already saddled. I feed Crazy Eyes a dish full of grain and then I take her to the creek for some water.

There's a small buckskin horse and a brown horse with white spots tied to a hitching rail. Both of them have pack saddles and two giant burlap bags Gene calls panniers attached to the wood of the saddles.

When I've mounted Crazy Eyes, Mike hands me a lead rope that connects to the brown horse's halter and gives Gene the other.

Gene leads, and I keep Crazy Eyes just behind the buckskin. Together, the four horses form a sort-of train that's leaving the station. The moon has already set, so the only things to lead us are the stars and Gene's memory.

We don't say anything. I just listen to the steady rhythm of the horses.

Every so often, I'll see a bright spark appear beneath the buckskin's hoof, like she stepped on a firecracker. I hear the yipping of coyotes and I see my first shooting star. I make a wish that neither of us gets eaten. That everyone will get to see who I've become.

Even though it's got to be below zero degrees, Gene doesn't seem as sick as he did before. This place is like medicine to him.

We ride through Fish Creek, then North Fork, then Purdy. By the time we reach the place where we climbed on foot yesterday, I can't feel my hands.

The sky begins to brighten just over the hills, and I smile. Warmth is on its way.

Instead of going on foot, we let the horses take us up the hill. Crazy Eyes's head bobs sharply as she gets each step placed, jostling me in my saddle.

Just as we reach the top, the sun peeks out, and light fills the valley and shines onto the trees we entered yesterday. There's no way the horses are going to fit through these woods while we're riding, so we get off and walk with them until the trees and brush get too thick for them to pass. If nothing has eaten my elk, it should be just another hundred feet up this hill.

We tie the horses to the trees and carry the panniers. My elk is still here, completely intact. This time I do feel relieved, that maybe all this is normal and I've been freaking out over nothing.

I can't believe I'm this hard-core. Karen said that in Texas, hunters shoot animals from pickup trucks inside fenced ranches. They use chain saws to quarter the meat. And they barely break a sweat.

There are no fences here. Not a single human around for miles. This really is the wilderness. But I'm not scared like I was yesterday, even though we'll be hauling at least five hundred pounds of meat out of the woods.

Gene reaches into a pannier and pulls out all the tools we'll need to quarter the elk — a hatchet and a mallet. That's it. He says, "You start with the head and I'll remove the hooves."

On Gene's instructions, I clear away the fur and muscle

with his skinning knife. Then, using his tools, I chip away at the bone until I get the head free. There's a deep, burning feeling in my biceps I've never felt before.

Gene throws the hooves onto the gut pile. He shows me how to split the body in half and then into quarters. I enter the cavity and sever the spine down the middle, being careful not to let the hatchet slide off center. This is the hardest part, but after a few tries while gritting my teeth, I splice the body into four heavy sections.

I fall on my butt and admire my accomplishment. The remnants no longer look like an animal. At this point, it's just meat.

We drag the first two panniers with the elk's head and hindquarters toward the horses and tie them onto the wood of the buckskin's saddle. Out of the corner of my eye, I see Crazy Eyes start neighing and jerking her head.

"Hey, cool it," I say.

She pulls at the tree, bending it back. Pine needles fall to the ground.

"I said cool it!"

Now all the horses are neighing and freaking out.

Gene looks up the hill. A dark, squat form is moving toward the rest of my elk. It has a large shoulder hump, a concave snout, and two round ears on its wide head.

A billow of steam rises from its mouth.

Gene says in a calm but stern voice, "We have to go."

The thing appears from the shadows, and it's a big dog. No, it's a *very* big dog with one thousand pounds of muscle.

No, he's a giant linebacker hunched down on all fours. His face is scarred and, my God, he's so fat.

No, it's a she. Her fur is blond, almost the color of sand. She's the one who tore down a tent and ate two hunters from Ohio.

It's Sandy.

She sneaks slow, with her head down. She's coming for my elk. She sniffs the gut pile and grunts. Despite what Gene told me about grizzly bears — that they like their meat nasty — she goes for the front quarters, leaving the entrails untouched.

"Hey!" I holler, and then I smack my hands over my mouth.

The bear rears onto her hind legs — she's at least eight feet tall — and sniffs the air. Her face is expressionless and huge. Her legs are as thick as tree trunks. Panic races through me, and I freeze.

I can't feel my arms or legs. I can't feel anything.

My throat closes and I can't breathe.

The buckskin breaks free from the tree, taking the hindquarters and the head of my elk with her.

"Get on your horse," Gene says.

I still can't breathe. I need to breathe!

The grizzly sways her head side to side and then woofs. She gets down on all fours and tears another chunk out of my elk's leg.

Grizzlies can run thirty miles an hour. Gene and I will both be dead in a matter of seconds.

I force myself to breathe.

Air rushes into my lungs and this is not real. The bear is not real. I'm not really here, and this is just a game where I get double points for head shots.

My eyes focus on Crazy Eyes, and even though she's bucking and pulling at the tree, I get my rifle out of the scabbard.

Sandy charges at me, breaking everything in her path. Her massive haunches move so quickly that I don't know what's happening. I drop my rifle and I close my eyes and I'm going to die.

She stops short. I open my eyes. I'm still alive. The bear stands no more than twenty feet away, opening and closing her mouth, clacking her teeth.

The bear's empty black eyes stare into mine. She roars. It's so brutal and fierce that I can feel it in my bones.

This is real. The blood on her ragged teeth. The stink of death. The claws.

This is not a game I can reset.

Sandy huffs and returns to my elk. With her paw pressed against the open cavity, she tears off another piece.

"Tyson," Gene says from behind, "get on your horse."

My legs are trembling so hard. I wrap my hand around the saddle's horn and place one foot in the stirrup when Crazy Eyes does a back kick and knocks me down. The bear is still standing by my elk. Watching me. Crazy Eyes is panicking so hard, the knot tying her to the tree is almost undone.

We are the next headline.

"Boy and Grandfather Mauled to Death in Wyoming."

Gene lets the brown horse go. He smacks Ellie in the face, and she calms down just long enough for him to mount her. He looks at me. I have to do the same.

Crazy Eyes has exhausted herself pulling at the tree and doesn't yet realize the knot is loose. I have to get on her before she leaves without me.

I smack her hard in the face, the rope in my other hand. "Calm down."

She writhes her neck but stays steady. I get one foot in, swing my other foot around, and then I kick her good in the belly.

Like a bullet from a gun, she shoots through the woods with Gene right behind. I'm hugging Crazy Eyes's neck tight, twigs breaking across my face. We enter the clearing, gallop up and over the hill, and my arms begin to weaken. My butt gets higher off the saddle with every downward stride.

I take my feet out of the stirrups because my arms and my body can't take any more. And so I let go, slamming against the ground. I go tumbling down the hill. My hand reaches out and latches on to the stem of a sagebrush, pulling the plant out. I claw into the dirt until my fingernails scrape across a lodged rock.

I scream. And . . . I stop. Dizzy, I stumble to my feet and search for Gene. All I see is Crazy Eyes turning right onto the trail and vanishing beyond the hill.

"Gene?" I look all around. "Gene!"

The only response is the echo of my voice. Then the silence returns.

"Gene!"

Oh, God, he's gone. I'm by myself. I look up to the top of the hill. He was right behind me.

A form appears at the summit, and relief sets in.

But it's not Gene.

The grizzly bear charges toward me at full speed.

CHAPTER 23

Beneath a Heavy and Warm Shadow

Don't run. Don't run. Don't run.

Play dead. Curl up in a ball. Put my hands around the back of my neck.

The bear charges and I don't see her, but she's an avalanche that gets louder. Closer. The ground trembles.

I peek. The bear slides past me. She can't control her momentum.

She looks at me from below, panting, and huffs her way back up. Her steps are slow.

Don't scream. Don't fight her. Don't do anything.

She's here! Oh, my God, I can feel her shadow. It's heavy and warm, and I will not scream. I swallow it down, and it's like shards of hot glass in my throat. My heart is pounding so heavily and it's way too loud.

Shut up, you stupid heart! *Shut up!*

A weight presses onto my back—her paw. The points of her claws touch me, but they don't sink in. She doesn't move for a thousand years and then she smacks me.

I go rolling.

Stay curled up. Keep my hands around my neck.

There isn't anything else I can do, and if I die, maybe I was meant to die in this place.

And then something stops me. A willow bush. I'm not dead yet.

I should say something. I need my last words, even if no one's around to hear them. What should they be?

I make one eye open. The path is three feet away. And then I hear a glorious sound—a thundering blast from Gene's rifle, and it's so loud it has to scare Sandy away.

It doesn't scare her away because there was no gunshot. It was only in my head.

The grizzly bear is breathing the smell of death onto me.

I love you, Mom. I love you, Dad. And Gene. And Bright. And I never got to know you very well, but I would have been a good boyfriend for you, Karen. Heck, I even love you too, Ashley.

No words come out of my mouth.

Sandy paws at me again, and something sharp slides down my back and I'm just whatever about it.

Just go ahead and get it over with. I'm not here to hurt you or your cubs. And I've done everything I was supposed to do, but if you're going to kill me anyways, there's nothing I can do to stop you.

She grunts. It's a frustrated sound, like she's bored with me.

A hundred years of her tired, atrocious breathing pass, and a warm glob of drool lands on my face.

Then it just comes to me. "Why do you have to be so mean?" I whisper, so quiet I'm not sure I say anything at all. Those will be my last words.

I'm going to die being my stupid whatever self, a smile on my face. Maybe this is what happens just before you die — you get delirious. This is something beyond being scared.

I remain perfectly still.

I don't know how much time has passed, but I open my eyes and see no sign of the bear. Where did she go? Am I dead? I have to be — this doesn't feel like the same world. And all the colors are different. Everything is bright and disorienting.

Sandy didn't eat me. Why didn't she eat me?

I try and stand, but my left leg buckles. I look at my hand. There is no nail on my middle finger, just a red-and-white fleshy patch dripping with blood. But nothing hurts.

The front of my jeans is soaked in pee.

"Gene?"

He could be lying dead on the side of the trail.

I hobble to my feet and hurry toward North Fork with a gimpy left leg.

"Gene?" I say it louder.

I pass the bend. On the opposite side of the creek and sprawled across the rocks is this soaked, frail old man. For a second, I think he really is dead.

"Gene!"

He looks at me. He struggles to get up, but he stumbles in the current.

"Tyson!" he cries. "I thought you were dead!"

I splash through the icy creek.

"I'm sorry," he says, his voice breaking. "I tried to turn my horse around, but I couldn't. I couldn't hold on, and she threw me off. I tried to come for you."

"I'm okay. Gene, look, everything's fine."

"We shouldn't have done this trip."

"What? Why?"

"Why? It nearly killed you!"

I kneel beside him, the frigid water rushing around me. "Let me help you up." I sling his arm around my shoulder. We're both about to collapse back in, but I drag both of us onto land.

"Tyson, what happened to your back?"

His words bring to life a searing pain slicing across my skin. "Huh?" I try to look over my shoulder. "What is it?"

"The bear clawed you." He smacks me on the back of the head, hard. "What the hell were you doing, pulling out your rifle? You never do that! That's why that damn bear charged. You pissed her off good. Dummy."

I force a joke. "We could have gotten a grizzly head to hang up." It comes out like a whimper.

"I'd rather have *your* stupid head on the wall."

"I'm sorry, Gramps."

He sighs and puts his arm around my shoulder, bringing me in for a hug. And he keeps me there. He says, "Look at me. I'm a useless old fart, and I couldn't control my horse. And I want your grandmother back. And for Pete's sake, I don't want to have to piss every goddamn thirty minutes."

He wipes his face and says, "It goes by so fast. One minute you're in middle school, then the next you're all by yourself in a nursing home."

I can't think of anything that will make him feel better or change the situation. I'm not wise. I don't know what it's like to be old.

I don't really know much of anything.

Into his jacket I say, "What are we going to do about the horses?"

"They know how to get home. They go where the food is." He glances at my back again. "We ought to get Nancy to check you out. Those claw marks look deep."

"Will it scar?"

He nods. "You're going to look like a badass."

I give a tired wink. "That's because I am."

We hobble toward the ranch, soaked and freezing, and my mind is really blank and clear, but I'm thinking about *everything*. What am I going to be like when I'm twenty years old? Will I be working at McDonald's, or will I be in college? Am I going to get married when I'm thirty, divorce when I'm forty, retire when I'm sixty?

Will I live in a nursing home when I'm seventy-seven?

I could die tomorrow.

He goes, "By the way, you made two mistakes today."

"What's the other one?"

"You called me Gramps."

My face tingles, all warm and weird. But it wasn't a mistake. I know who he is. He's the same person he's always been — he's family. He's my grandfather.

CHAPTER 24

BFFs

The ATV comes hauling up to the property line. Mike is driving and Nancy is sitting behind him, her arms around his waist.

"What happened?" Nancy says. "You boys are drenched."

The sun is high and it's got to be sixty degrees out and Gramps and I are still alive. Everything is fantastic.

Mike says, "You guys didn't come across Sandy, did you?"

If I tell them where she's at, then the Forest Service will kill her. A grizzly bear — the coolest animal to ever exist — will die because of me. Should I say anything? I mean, Sandy let me live, and it's only right that I return the favor. But who's to say she won't hurt someone else?

Can't there be a third option?

I breathe in through my nose and out my mouth, and I can't regret this decision. I say, "We spotted her between Purdy and Hackamore."

Stunned, Mike says, "We'll get on the CB and call it in. You guys need a lift?"

Gramps looks at me and says, "What's another two hundred yards?"

"And don't mention our names," I add. I don't want Dad finding out through a newspaper blurb that I lied to him.

When the rumbling ATV retreats, Gramps says, "You did the right thing, telling them about Sandy."

"It doesn't feel like the right thing."

Gramps puts his arm around me and says, "Welcome to adulthood."

God, being an adult sucks. You have to make all these horrible decisions. If you don't kill a majestic grizzly bear whose only fault was that she loved her cubs, she could attack someone else. If you don't screw over your Taylor Swift–loving best friend, you'll never hear the end of it from your teammates. If you don't spend the rest of your life in a nursing home, your kidneys could fail tomorrow.

It's funny — I'm not mad at anyone anymore. We're all doomed to be adults.

We pass the wooden fence and the orange sign and

reenter civilization. I want to ask Gramps about all those secret grown-up conversations he had with Mom and Dad before they put him in the nursing home. But today's been heavy enough.

I say, "Hey, Gramps, how old were you when you got your first kiss?"

"Uh, that would be Dorothy McCoy, the homecoming queen from Abilene."

"I thought you met her fifty-nine years ago."

"Good memory."

"But that would make you eighteen."

"Seventeen, actually. A week before my eighteenth birthday."

"You got your first kiss when you were seventeen?" My whole world tilts. I always pictured Gramps flirting in his high chair.

He says, "I was a pretty awkward kid. All my friends were playing baseball and meeting up with girls, but I wasn't what you'd call athletic, and I was downright terrified of girls."

"Wow, really? I guess you *are* my grandfather."

He smiles.

"So how'd you change?" I say.

"My folks, my three sisters, and I were in Texas to visit

my grandparents, and I met Dorothy waitressing at a burger joint. I knew I would regret it if I didn't ask her out. I took her to the county fair. I called her my little Texas bear. Oh, and Tyson?"

"Yes, sir?"

"The bear thing? Calling them a Texas bear or a sweetie bear? Don't stop. Girls love it."

The buckskin is standing outside the barn, eating from a flake of hay. Her pack saddle and panniers have been removed and are sitting on the ground. My elk's head is still strapped to the saddle.

"Hey, at least we managed to get the rack," I say.

Gramps unties the head from the saddle and pulls a set of pliers from his multitool. "Only two North American animals produce ivory. One of them is the walrus." He rolls up his sleeves, pulls back the elk's upper lip, and latches on to a shiny tooth near the front. With a bunch of firm wiggles, his wrist and arm muscles tightening, he gets the tooth free. The root is deep and covered in gore.

He puts it in my palm and says, "The other is the elk."

"This is actual ivory?"

"Yes, sir. Every elk's got two of them. I know of a place just south of Jackson that can clean them up for us." He removes the other one. "Cool, huh?"

"Very."

It takes Nancy about an hour to dress the gashes on my back. And as I sit there with my shirt off and the alcohol stinging my wounds, I think about Brighton. Even though he's got more muscle than I do, he isn't stronger than me. He sucks at kicking, he's desperate to have people like him, and he puts makeup over his zits. Oh, and he's a raging yamhole.

I wouldn't want to hang out with anyone else.

I'll still be friends with him. I mean, life's too short to hold stupid grudges. But I'm not going to let Bright off the hook for telling his football buddies my secrets. There's only one punishment to fit the crime.

"She must have liked you," Mike says.

I look up. "Huh?"

"Sandy. Looks like she was just playing with you. Like a cat does with a toy mouse. She must've felt a bond."

"Just call me Grizzly Kid," I say, paying homage to Timothy Treadwell the Grizzly Man, and get a laugh out of everyone.

We don't have time for hanging out — it's Sunday afternoon, and I have to get home so I can get some studying in, even though the whole concept of school seems so . . . civilized.

I get cleaned up in the ranch's icy shower and put on a fresh set of clothing, tossing the dirty stuff away. We thank Mike and Nancy for everything and then load the elk meat and the head into the bed of the truck.

We get back on the Gros Ventre Road. It's so different from the horrifying and winding dirt trail we came in on, even though it's the same road. It turns out it's actually pretty and rustic and not scary at all. We pass vast pastures filled with horses, and mountains of different colors. We drive tire-deep through four creeks. At one point on a nearby hill, a pack of pronghorn antelope stares us down for a minute before we get too close and they gallop away. Gene flags down a pickup truck that's got a dead black bear in the bed. The driver shares his hunting stories and talks about how afraid he was that he'd run into Sandy.

I yawn, not because I'm not interested. I'm just really, really, really tired.

Gramps pulls over at a lookout point where hundreds of feet beneath us is a massive lake. A whole forest of treetops is poking out of the water.

"That's Slide Lake," he says while taking a pee off the cliff. "Great place for trout fishing. Back in the 1920s, a massive landslide blocked off the river and flooded the entire area. Beautiful, isn't it?"

It's a perfectly blue day, and in the distance the white-capped Grand Tetons watch over us. This is a place I'll want to take my kids and my grandkids to.

Somewhere before we reach the main highway, I pass out, and I don't wake up again until the truck comes to a stop and Gramps shifts into park. The sun is already setting.

We're back at the nursing home in Rock Springs. Everything we just did—the horseback riding, the elk hunt, the bear attack—feels like a distant dream.

"What about the meat?" I say.

"I left it with a processor back in Jackson."

"Really?"

"I didn't want to wake you. Now, either they can ship it all to Rock Springs, or we can split it fifty-fifty and they'll deliver to the house."

"Then Mom and Dad will know we went hunting."

"It's your call."

Yeah, there really isn't any debate. Dad will say I'm grounded until I'm eighteen, but he'll forget or lose interest in a few weeks. Hopefully.

I say, "Let's do it. What about the rack?"

"It's your elk. Besides, I got what I came for."

He reaches into his coat pocket and pulls out the two

elk ivories, already polished up and fashioned into simple necklaces. "I stopped by my friend Rod Husky's shop in Hoback Junction. He's a jeweler — fixed these up for us in an hour." He hands me one and says, "One for you. One for me."

I put it on and check myself out in the vanity mirror. Not gonna lie, I look hot. "These will be like our BFF necklaces."

"What's BFF?"

"Best friends forever."

Gramps smiles and laughs, and as hard as he's trying not to cry, his eyes are getting red and sad. "I'm going to miss you so much. I really wish I could live with you and the family, but . . ."

But I already know. There's no going back to the way things were before. His broken kidneys aren't magically going to fix themselves. Maybe if we were rich, he'd be at home in his reclining chair watching *Wheel of Fortune* and *Jeopardy!* while his home dialysis equipment pumped away. And then he could go about his daily routine, living his golden years with his family by his side.

The Sunrise Village Nursing Home is his new life.

I say, "I'm going to visit all the time. I *bear swear.*" I hold my hands out and make them into claws.

He takes his claws and interlocks them with mine. And we growl.

It's dark by the time Mom and Dad arrive at the nursing home. They ask a hundred questions about our trip to the Targhee National Forest, but I don't say much. I'm too tired to lie and too tired to tell the truth.

The five of us have dinner at Red Robin. As Mom and Dad are going on about their adventures in Rock Springs, I just sit there, taking the skin on the top of my hand and folding it together so it's all wrinkly like I'm some seventy-seven-year-old man who fought in Korea, saved a beautiful woman and her son from a deadbeat, worked at a feed and tractor supply store for over thirty years, and loved everyone.

We drop Gramps off at the nursing home. We each take turns giving him a hug and a kiss and then we say our good-byes. I want to tell him that he's going to get better and that maybe someday he'll live with us again. But I can't lie to him. All I can do is say, "I love you, Gramps."

CHAPTER 25

The Latest Issue of
Better Homes and Gardens

When I get home from school on Tuesday, there's a blurb from the newspaper cut out and taped to my door:

Killer Grizzly Bear Is Found and Slain

The 25-year-old bear known by locals as Sandy, who killed two hunters from Ohio, was found in the Bridger-Teton National Forest on Monday by the Forest Service, who then put her down. Autopsy revealed human remains as well as elk carrion, most likely a recent kill from a hunter.

"I found that this morning," Ashley says, standing outside her bedroom door. "Thought you'd be interested."

"Thanks, Sis."

"You didn't see her at all, did you?"

"The bear? Nah, no luck."

"It's a shame the bear had to die."

I nod understandingly, but what the heck? She's wearing my belt with the rattlesnake buckle! I was looking all over my room for it this morning.

She goes, "I'm really glad you and Gramps got to go on that trip."

"Nice belt."

"Huh?" She looks down. "Yeah, I think I look kinda cute with it."

The truth is, it does look good on her.

I say, "You keep it."

"Really? I was going to ask you if I could wear it next weekend to Rock Springs."

"I also have a couple of flannels that don't fit me anymore."

"Gee, thanks, Tyson. There's nothing I want more than your disgusting old shirts." She wraps her arms around me and sarcastically says, "Oh, how I love my big brother. He's so generous."

"Gross. Get off." I squirm away and open my door.

"Old flannels. You've got such good taste. Come here!"

She tackles me onto the floor. I'm laughing, and then she starts laughing, too, and wow, her breath reeks.

I go, "Dude. You smell like McNuggets. Get off."

"Hey." She playfully smacks me across the cheek. "That's not nice."

My phone beeps.

"Who is it?" Ashley says.

"Nobody. Get out of here."

She snatches the phone from me. "You got a text? From a *girl*? Tyson!" She acts like this is the biggest deal. "Who's Karen?"

"Don't worry about it." I shove her out of my room, lock the door, and hurry to check my phone.

Karen wrote: *We still on for karaoke?*

I message back: *See you in ten, karenbear.*

I wait a minute for her to respond. My entire body tingles with anticipation. And then finally: *lol okay tysonbear :)*

I grab my bike from the garage. For an early November day, it's surprisingly warm and bright out. I'm wearing my Taylor Swift T-shirt untucked for a change, and it feels good having the breeze around me.

Bright's bike is locked up in front of Party Fiesta Karaoke, and I put mine next to it. There isn't anyone inside except for him, Mika, and Karen, and an extra-large pizza, which is solid. But the stage is empty, which is not solid.

"Hey, guys," I say, and take a seat next to Karen. She's staring at my elk ivory necklace. "You got supreme pizza. That's totally yam."

Karen says, "You guys keep saying that. What on earth do 'yam' and 'yamhole' mean?"

I've gotten much better at my sexy eyes. I say, "Whatever you want them to mean."

Unfazed, Karen responds with "Is that some Colorado thing?"

Mika shakes her head. "No, it's some Tyson and Bright thing."

I say, "We need to hurry up and eat, because at six o'clock, me and Bright purge."

"Now, what does *that* mean?" Karen says.

"We're each going to drink a jug of prune juice," Brighton says sadly.

After we finish our pizza, me and Bright take the stage and tell the deejay to put on our song: "Mean" by Taylor Swift.

I say into the mike, "All right, ladies and gents out there, here's a classic by Pizza Bear."

And then Bright says, "And Booger Bear Five Thousand."

When we get to the chorus, my voice cracks like some-one just took a claw to my throat and sliced it open. I stop for a moment and my face gets warm, but Bright doesn't laugh. He continues to sing as if nothing happened.

We do two more songs together, and after convincing the girls for five minutes, we get them onstage, but they're pretty much just laughing and blurting out random words.

Karen slings her arm across my shoulder and then, just as the song finishes, something soft touches the corner of my lips. I don't even know what just happened until a moment later when I look at her. Her eyes are so bright they seem to be smiling. And then it hits me — I just got my first kiss.

What is it like to fall in love? I don't know, but whatever this is, it's pretty neat.

So I'm thirteen, I just got kissed, and a grizzly bear practically mauled me, but I still don't feel like a man.

Six o'clock is fast approaching. Bright and I need to get to my home ASAP. So we race our bikes back, and I beat him by a solid fifteen seconds.

He sits across from me at the kitchen table, huffing as he reads the label on the jug in front of him, an awesome hint of fear in his voice: "Country Orchard Prune Juice."

My fingers are rapping against the side of my jug and I'm staring at the bird clock above the sink.

"Don't back out now," I say, because the look on his face says it all. "This is how you will pay for your crimes."

"But why would anyone do this?"

"You can thank me later."

So in fifty-four seconds, it will be six o'clock.

Tick.

In fifty-three seconds, the Canada goose will honk.

Tick.

In fifty-two seconds, Bright and I will each be chugging a liter of prune juice to completion. Who will get to the bathroom first? Who will lock the door on the other?

This is a done deal.

The Canada goose honks, and I chug my liter down without even flinching. I slam my empty jug on the table, burp, and check the clock. It only took me thirty seconds. Bright, on the other hand, is gagging and forcing down his just deserts. He gives up about halfway through.

"I don't know how on earth you do that," he says, making a face. "So now what?"

"Now we watch *Wheel of Fortune*."

We go into the living room and he sits on the sofa, and I

explain to him what's about to happen. There will be some sweating, a little bit of crying, and a lot of toilet paper.

I take a seat in Gramps's reclining chair and turn on *Wheel of Fortune.*

Bright doesn't say much for the next hour. I can feel his fear. He's barely paying any attention to *Wheel of Fortune* or *Jeopardy!* Doesn't he know that the whole point of pruning is to sit back and relax?

So we both eye the clock again, waiting for the final-Jeopardy question.

The category is: The Revolutionary War.

The answer is: *On April 18, 1775, Paul Revere warned his countrymen that the British were coming, prompting this battle, the very first in the American Revolutionary War.*

Before they even begin to play the final-Jeopardy music, I shout out, "What is the Battle of Lexington and Concord? Yeah, I win! The Americans defeat the British yet again."

"I really have to go," Bright says. He's clenching every muscle in his body.

"Patience," I say.

When seven o'clock comes around, Bright and I both jump up and race to the bathroom. I stiff-arm him, holding him back as I close the door and turn the lock.

There we go. *Now* I feel like a man.

Bright is pounding on the door.

"Come on, Tyson!"

"Why don't you stop by Mr. Privett's place? I'm sure he won't mind."

"How long are you going to be in there?"

"Dude. We have a new issue of *Better Homes and Gardens* in here. It's going to be a while."

I hear him run away. I already know that after this he's going to be a changed man. Maybe we won't be ten years old again, but that's okay. I can still find newer and better ways to have fun with him. Even if it's at his expense.

I've learned something. Something I'll tell my kids, and my kids will pass on to their kids — revenge is a dish best served with prunes.

roar.

ACKNOWLEDGMENTS

Thanks to my agent, John M. Cusick, for believing in and loving this story as much as I do; my agent's agent, Scott Treimel; Brendan Rien and Mike Henry, for the ridiculous Wyoming adventure that helped inspire this story; and my beta readers: Sage Collins, Helen Sedwick, and Michael Ware. A special shout-out to Rae Mariz for reading all my manuscripts (good, bad, atrocious) and never being afraid to throw some much appreciated punches in my direction. Thanks to the Musers, for always being a source of encouragement, motivation, and GIFs. And of course, my editor, Joan Powers, and the team at Candlewick Press for taking a chance on me and my little story.

Here's hoping that this book will score me a date with Taylor Swift. Just throwing that out there. . . .